Lipstick Killah 3

Lock Down Publications and Ca$h
Presents
Lipstick Killah 3
A Novel by *Mimi*

Lock Down Publications
P.O. Box 870494
Mesquite, Tx 75187

Visit our website @
www.lockdownpublications.com

Lock Down Publications
Like our page on Facebook: Lock Down Publications @
www.facebook.com/lockdownpublications.ldp
Cover design and layout by: **Dynasty Cover Me**
Book interior design by: **Shawn Walker**
Edited by: Jill Alicea

Stay Connected with Us!

Text **LOCKDOWN** to 22828 to stay up-to-date with new releases, sneak peaks, contests and more…

Thank you.

Acknowledgments

First things first, I want to give all the glory to the man upstairs. If he hadn't shown me this gift at a young age, I don't know where or what I would be doing today.

I have to thank my family and my kids for believing in me when I didn't believe in myself. I am my toughest critic and I always doubt myself, but they have been there rooting me on since the beginning of time. When I didn't want to do it, they pushed me. I love you all!

To the awesome readers, thank you for being there and reading every messed up thought I've had in my head while writing this. I can't thank you all enough for rocking with me. I hope that I can still deliver for each and every one of you! I love y'all and the way y'all support me as well.

To my LDP fam, y'all are honestly dope. There are too many of us to name, but just know that the support will always be real and there until the very end.

To my publisher Cash, thank you. I was at a low when you wrote that comment and invited me over to join LDP! The best decision I've made in my entire industry life. I cannot thank you enough!

Last but not least, to the naysayers, doubters, and the ones that just knew that I would be nothing, FUCK YOU!

Mimi

Chapter One

Dim lights, sterile air, beeping machines, and death lingering in the air…Hospitals had become the norm for Reign and Senaj. Each time, the visit would be more complicated than before. While Senaj was grateful that he had his baby girl, the love of his life was in danger. The amount of pain that filled Senaj's chest was unimaginable. Almost losing his child and his future wife in the same day could have sent him into the cuckoo's nest.

"What do you mean she flat-lined?" Akuchi asked.

"For five minutes, she was dead. They got her back, but now they placed her in a medically-induced coma just so that she could heal better without any extra stresses," Senaj said.

"Bro, you know she's gonna be fine," Akuchi stated. Even though he wasn't sure that was true, he had to believe it just enough to make sure his brother believed it too.

Jackie walked up to Senaj and gave him a hug, causing Senaj to bury his head into her neck and silently cry. Jackie tried to keep it together, but as she felt his body shake in her arms, she couldn't hold hers in any longer. Senaj wasn't the only one who was afraid of losing Reign. Although the cousins were just getting to know each other, they had grown to love each other and create a bond that was inseparable.

"When can you see Zariyah?" Jackie asked when she pulled away from Senaj. They wiped their eyes and sat down next to Akuchi and Jamori, who was holding baby K.B.

"I'm a horrible father already. I didn't even think about asking the doctor that. Only thing that was stuck in my mind was the fact that I could have lost Reign," Senaj sobbed.

"Cut that shit out right now. There is just too much going on. All you got to do is ask a doctor," Jackie said.

"Yeah, you're right."

Senaj got up and walked to the nurses' station. He asked to speak with a doctor. A few minutes passed, and a doctor came up to him. Luckily for him, the doctor was able to take him to see his baby girl. His heart boomed against his chest with each step that he took towards the NICU.

"We have managed to stabilize your daughter's breathing machine, but the good thing is that she is showing brain activity. Our plan is to wean her off oxygen for longer periods of time. Of course, we want her to not need it at all. She has a feeding tube for the moment. As we slowly take her off the oxygen, we will try to get her to latch onto a bottle."

"Okay," Senaj simply replied as he tried to keep track of everything the doctor was saying. Before he was allowed inside of the NICU, the doctor told Senaj to put on a surgical gown, shoe protectors, and a mask. With each passing step, he looked down at each baby in their incubators.

"Here is your baby girl. Right now, you can't hold her, but soon she will be able to come out of the incubator for skin to skin contact," the doctor said.

Senaj was in awe and couldn't help but to be proud. He said a silent prayer for Reign and Zariyah for a speedy recovery. He needed both of them home, sooner rather than later. He apologized to Reign under his breath, hoping that she would understand that he would be spending the night with Zariyah.

Two weeks later...

Senaj was finally going to trial for the cop who shot him. It was all over the news, and the department even offered him a settlement. He turned it down due to his lawyer telling him not to take it, that he could get him way more than the fifty thousand that they were trying to offer. For Senaj, it wasn't about the money. It was about bringing awareness to racism with cops shooting unarmed black men. It was becoming normal, and it wasn't sitting well with him and many black people across America. All he wanted was justice.

By his side were his parents, his brother, and the twins. He sat at the desk with his attorney as they listened to the racist cop's attorney say how Burke felt his life was in danger. This infuriated Senaj to the point where he almost lost his cool. His attorney told him to sit tight, and the fact that the jury was sixty percent black was in his favor. Although everything appeared to be going in his favor, he knew that there was a possibility that something could go wrong. The black people that were on the jury could be Uncle Tom's, and his whole case and the justice that he was trying to get would be pointless.

"Court is adjourned until tomorrow." The judge banged his gavel, and everyone rose from their seats.

Senaj felt his father's hand on his shoulder, silently letting Senaj know that everything would be okay.

"I have good news," Senaj's attorney whispered as they spilled into the hallway of the court building.

"What's that?"

"Burke's partner, Dillard, the one that was on the scene, is going to testify tomorrow. I had an inside source tell me that they overheard the captain threaten to fire Dillard if he did testify. I have this in a written statement, and even Dillard doesn't know. It will protect him just in case - you know, like a thank you because you didn't have to type of thing. My source told me that he has quit since the captain threatened him and is looking to go to a less racist district."

"Okay, good. If anything changes, please give me a call. My daughter is coming home from the hospital and I have to finish getting things ready for her arrival," Senaj said while shaking his lawyer's hand.

As always, they parted ways and went in separate directions. The lawyer went out the front with many reporters to willingly answer their eager questions while Senaj and his family went through the exit that didn't have any.

The ride back to Senaj's place was a quiet one. Senaj's thoughts were always on Zariyah and Reign. All his praying had worked and one of his ladies were coming home. No dependency on oxygen, but they were sending Zariyah home with some just in case. They were going to keep a close eye on her in her first year of living and gradually pull back as they saw her progression. Now Senaj just had to work on getting Reign home.

They entered Senaj's apartment one by one, each exhausted from the day's events. Senaj went right into the room that Kahlil and Zariyah would be sharing and took a seat in the rocking chair. He closed his eyes, as he wanted to enjoy that moment of peace and quiet.

"Senaj?" a soft voice called from the doorway.

He knew who it was automatically. His mother's voice was the only that could calm the thundering in his chest besides Reign's.

"Yes, Mama?" Senaj asked, opening his eyes.

"Can we talk?" she asked.

"Of course," Senaj replied. He got up from the rocking chair and let his mother have his seat. He sat at her feet and put his head on her lap like he used to do when he was a little boy.

"Your father and I were talking and we both agreed that when Zariyah is cleared to travel, the both of you should come stay with us."

That was something that Senaj wasn't expecting. He thought that she was going to give him a few words to at least make him feel better in his situation.

"What?" he questioned, removing his head from her lap.

His mother's face was filled with desperation as she said, "It wouldn't be for long. Until you find a job and your own place."

"Mama, let me get this straight. You want me to take my daughter and move her miles away from her mother – who, might I add, died for five minutes while bringing her into this world, and is still in a coma healing from delivering her. You want me to leave my son - "

"He is not your son!"

"I adopted him, Mom, so you know what that makes us? Father and son! Whether you like it or not. How would you like it if my father - your husband - would have taken Akuchi and me and left you after you had given birth to us?" Senaj asked. He was enraged, and he didn't want to sound like he was being disrespectful, because that was the last thing that he wanted his mother to think. But she was pushing his limits.

Zain jumped up from her seat on the rocking chair. She spat, "Regarde ton ton!"

By this time the others had gathered at the room door. Senaj said, "Mama, I'm a grown man. I refuse to watch my tone, especially when you are asking me to leave my family."

"You call her your family, but look at everything that has gone on with you since you've met her! You should have just stayed with Christina!" his mother yelled.

Jackie turned to Akuchi and whispered, "Who the fuck is Christina?"

Akuchi eyed her and said, "Nobody."

"I should have stayed with Christina? Funny thing is, Mom, she turned to drugs, robbed me, and broke my heart beyond measures imaginable. No thank you!" Senaj yelled.

"That's it! It's final! You will be moving as soon as my granddaughter is cleared to travel!"

"Like hell! She may be your granddaughter, but she's my child! Straight from my ball sack!"

"Assez!" Akachi's voice boomed. He had heard and seen enough.

"Oh shit," Jackie whispered.

Akuchi had heard enough. He knew that once his father jumped in, whatever he said was final, despite what or how anyone felt. He turned around and walked away and even though the nosy in them wanted to stay and listen, Jackie and Jamori followed Akuchi, and had no choice but to hear from Senaj what happened later.

$$***$$

Senaj was just leaving court when he got the call from Reign's doctor letting him know that she had woken up. He had planned on going home to spend time with Zariyah and Kahlil. It was October, and soon the weather would start to change, and he wanted them to get as much fresh air as they could stand. He called Jackie and asked if she could keep the kids a little while longer as he ran a quick errand. He didn't want to let anyone know the news yet until he laid eyes on her himself.

As he drove to Jamaica Hospital, he thought about his day in court. The jury unanimously came to the decision that Officer Burke was guilty and he would be spending ten to fifteen years in prison. The courtroom erupted in pandemonium and that's when, for the first time, Senaj knew how much support he had. Not only that, his lawyer put in motion to begin the process of suing the police department.

Senaj arrived at the hospital and raced through to find out where she was. A nurse told him that she had been moved to a recovery room and gave him the directions. As he made it to her room, his heart pounded in his chest as the anticipation of seeing Reign awake for the first time in three weeks. His palms were sweaty, and he was pretty sure that there was sweat forming under his underarms. He opened the door and almost went into cardiac arrest at what was in front of him.

Announcing his presence, he said, "Christina? What the fuck are you doing now?"

Mimi

Chapter Two

"Senaj, didn't I tell you what would happen if this woman was to come around me?" Reign asked. She was speaking to Senaj, but she was staring a hole through Christina.

"Yeah, you did," Senaj answered, running his hand down his face.

"Do you know how surprised I was to see her face instead of yours? Do you know how surprised I was that she was in here telling me how she's been fucking my man instead of my man telling me how my kids are doing? Do you know how surprised I was to hear that you are going to be a father yet again?" Reign yelled. For the first time, Senaj looked at Christina and noticed that she had a small, pregnant stomach. Senaj felt himself getting dizzy and couldn't believe how bad his luck had gotten.

"You didn't want to tell her, Senaj, and I thought that she needed to know," Christina said, trying to sound innocent.

"You sneaky, conniving bitch! How dare you? There is nothing to fucking tell," Senaj said, seething through his teeth. Christina was lucky Senaj was not a woman beater because if he was, she was going to regret what she had done once he beat her bloody throughout the hospital.

"So, you are telling me the night of her grandmother being shot, you didn't get drunk off your ass and text me to come get you from Smalls?" Christina asked, folding her arms across her chest with a smug look on her face.

Reign sat up and swung her feet over the bed, causing Christina to take a few steps back. She laughed a deep laugh and said to Senaj, "I knew you were lying, but I gave you the benefit of the doubt because you never gave me a reason to think you were a liar. I cannot believe this shit."

"Reign, if you would just listen to me. Yes, I lied. I got drunk with Rasheed and Polite. With all the shit that had been going on, I needed it. I sent a text message that I thought I was sending to you. The whole time, from when I sent the text up until Akuchi had told me about Nana…" Senaj's voice trailed off as he tried to figure out what else he could say to Reign. Getting his words together, he continued, "Reign, I'm sorry, I was drunk. And I know that isn't an excuse, but it's the truth. I would never ever do no shit like this to intentionally hurt you or put you in this predicament."

"See, Senaj, that's the thing, you didn't hurt me. You ignited a fire in me that I have never felt before, and I can't wait until these doctors discharge me. Both of y'all are dismissed."

"Reign - " Senaj began.

"No, Senaj. I will text you when they give me a day to let me out."

Christina smirked because at that moment, she felt like she was the victor of the two. She walked toward the door, a little too happy.

Senaj grabbed her by the arm and said, "Wipe that smile off your face. You will never have me. It will always be Reign. You don't know what you've done, and if you have that baby, I'm signing all of my rights away."

The color drained from Christina's face as she looked between Senaj and Reign. Senaj, without another word, walked out of the hospital room and Christina saw a sly smirk on Reign's face. Christina flew out of the hospital like a bat out of hell.

Reign sat on the bed once they were out of the room and began to cry and laugh at the same time. Reign told a bold-faced lie when she said that Senaj didn't hurt her. Her heart broke into pieces. But this was different than the heartbreak she had felt with Josiah. This was so very different. She didn't like it at all. She laid on the bed, clutching her heart as she allowed the tears to fall freely from her face onto her pillow.

***

"Senaj, you okay, bro?" Akuchi asked when Senaj had gotten into the house after visiting Reign.

Senaj loosened his tie and took it off, throwing it onto the couch. He went to go find Zariyah and Kahlil and when he found them, they were sleeping soundly in their cribs. He went back into the living room and took a seat on the couch.

"I've never wanted to lay my hands on someone so bad until this moment," Senaj said, clenching his hands open and shut.

"What do you mean? We saw the trial on TV and saw that you won. What's going on?"

"Where are the twins?" Senaj asked.

"They went to get some dinner."

"Reign is up."

"Word? When does she get to come home?"

"I don't know, and I think when she is able to, she won't be coming back here."

"Why?"

Senaj exhaled and pinched the bridge of his nose. He hated to have to repeat what happened, but he was at the point of not knowing what to do and he needed the help. He said, "Christina was in the room telling Reign every fucking thing. Oh, and she's pregnant."

The juice that Akuchi was drinking flew from his mouth and went halfway across the room. He said, "With your baby? Please, Senaj. Don't tell me you were that stupid."

"I was drunk. I wasn't in my right frame of mind. It wasn't about me being stupid. I honestly thought that she was Reign.

17

I told Christina if she was to keep the baby, I would be signing my rights away."

Akuchi stood up and went into the kitchen. He grabbed a beer from the fridge and sat back down. He slowly opened the beer and stared a hole in Senaj.

"So, because you were drunk and thought that she was Reign, that's an excuse for you to ditch a child that belongs to you? Because of a female? You get to be a deadbeat dad because you fucked up one time and you're afraid to lose Reign? Senaj, help me understand your reasoning, because you have absolutely no problem with taking care of Kahlil and he's neither yours nor hers. How do you get to leave this baby without a father?" Akuchi asked. Granted, he didn't have kids, but he despised men who left their kids without giving them a chance. He didn't want his brother to be one of those men, because Senaj wasn't built that way.

Senaj was speechless. No matter how selfish he wanted to be, he knew that his brother was right. He loved Reign with everything in him, but if he had to admit it, he had said what he said to Christina out of anger. His head began to hurt at all the hell that was unfolding.

Senaj said, "Since you have all of the answers, what do I do now?"

After taking a swig from his beer, Akuchi stood up and said, "That's for you to figure out. I can't always help you figure things out."

When Akuchi walked out of the living room, Jackie and Jamori came back with pizza. Zariyah began to cry, so Senaj went to go get her. He needed to be alone with his thoughts. He needed to figure things out before Reign came home.

Chapter Three

Finding out that her boyfriend, her man, the love her life, had cheated on her was the most devastating thing that could happen to her. Sure, almost losing her life and her child was challenging. But God was on her side and they both lived through it. But this...this was something that she didn't know if she could come back from.

Hours after Senaj had left, Reign signed herself out of the hospital. It went against doctor's orders, of course, but legally, they couldn't hold her. And if they tried, Reign already had a number that she wouldn't have a problem dialing to shut that shit down if need be. With everything in her, she wanted to just go home and see her kids, but she had something to do before she made it known that she was home - everyone except Jackie, who just so happened to pull up at the right moment. Reign climbed into the Escalade that Jackie had rented and they pulled off. Jackie snuck a look at Reign and smiled.

"I am so glad to have you back. I couldn't deal with being around those niggas anymore," Jackie said while laughing.

Reign sighed and said, "How are the kids? Especially Zariyah, because I know that she's had some complications."

"She's keeping everyone on their toes, and she has all of the men wrapped around her little fingers."

"I can't wait to see her," Reign said with a smile.

"Now that that's out of the way, please tell me what the hell is going on? Why are we riding out to Westchester County, and why couldn't I tell anyone that you signed out of the hospital? Everyone has been worried about you. Especially Senaj. That man took a leave from work and everything just so that he could be there with the kids."

Reign grew tired about hearing about Senaj. Everybody thought that he was just the good guy. Reign thought so too until she found out he cheated. Before the tears threatened to surface, she said to Jackie, "Senaj had everybody fooled. He's not as perfect as everyone thought he was."

"Reign, I - "

"Please, Jackie. I don't want to talk about Senaj. I need to focus on this task at hand."

Jackie looked at Reign again and decided to drop the issue - for now, anyway. Even though Reign didn't speak about it, Jackie knew exactly why Reign was upset. It seemed like Senaj wasn't listening to Akuchi's words and it was bothering him. So of course he turned to Jackie about the situation, and she was the one who told Akuchi to let him know that Senaj would have to figure it out on his own. She told Akuchi that he couldn't continue to hold his hand. It was time for Senaj to fix his own mistakes.

Forty minutes later, they made it to their destination. They pulled up to a one-story brick house that sat on top of a hill on Euclid Avenue in Ardsley, New York. They slowly crept past the house and noticed that all the lights were out, but there was a car in the driveway. Jackie continued a little further up the hill and made a U-turn. She parked the truck under a thick brush of leaves and branches that hung low from the trees. Reign climbed into the backseat and opened the duffel bag that Jackie had brought with them. Reign changed out of the scrubs that the hospital had let her leave in and into black jeans, a black hoodie, and all-black Converse's. She placed the hood on her head and grabbed her rose gold twins, placing them in her lower back. There was a fresh tube of her favorite Christian Louboutin lipstick at the bottom of the bag. A smile spread across her face and she couldn't be happier to see it.

When Reign was done and geared up, she looked at Jackie and nodded. They headed down the hill and to the house that they just passed by.

"Real quick, Reign. I know you may be hurt by what Senaj did, but he is a good man. What he did was a mistake, and you should really reconsider whatever you are thinking," Jackie said.

Reign sighed and said, "Jackie, have you ever been in love before?"

"No."

"Okay, so please don't try to give me advice on anything you don't know nothing about. I don't mean to sound harsh, but it is what it is."

Jackie didn't want to say anything else about the matter anyway. She had given her two cents and that's where it would end. In silence, they continued to walk to the house. They ascended the stairs and onto the porch. Reign walked up to the window and cupped her hands over her face to peer inside. It was complete darkness. Reign looked around the porch for a flowerpot, rug, or something that could give away that there could be a key hidden in it. There was none. Reign and Jackie walked around the side of the house and into the back. After walking onto the deck as quietly as they could, they saw multiple flowerpots and a rug. Reign signaled for Jackie to start looking for a spare key. Jackie found one seconds later under the rug and handed it to Reign.

"I know you don't have an attitude about this Senaj thing?" Reign whispered, looking at Jackie's furrowed brows.

"Hell no. That's your situation. I gave my opinion. I just want to know why the hell you haven't told me why we are here and whose house this is?" Jackie whispered.

"Remember the cop that shot Senaj?"

Jackie nodded.

"This is his house. Him shooting Senaj is why we are here."

Reign placed the key in the lock and the door opened effortlessly. They entered the kitchen and moved throughout the house, looking for Burke. For a male living alone, his house was surprisingly clean – that was, until they came across one of the bedroom doors. As they opened the door, the smell from the room almost knocked them back out onto the porch. They used their hands to try and mask the smell. It was a mixture of liquor, throw up, and old food. On the bed was Burke with pizza boxes, filth, and only God knows what else. There was barely any space to walk on the floor, but they managed to get through to the bed. Reign took one of her guns form the small of her back, and with the butt of the gun, she slammed it down hard on his dick and balls.

Pain ripped through Burke's body and he sat up, howling. "Shut your ass up," Reign said, aiming her gun at him.

"What the fuck? Who are you?" Burke asked. He was a bit drunk. He had been drinking since he had been found guilty. His sentencing day wasn't coming until the following week due to the judge giving him time to get his affairs in order. He didn't have anything to get in order, so he figured that he would spend his last free days drunk.

"Get your ass up and head to the living room," Reign barked. She wanted to be as far away from that room as possible.

Burke began to protest until he finally saw the gun that was damn near down his throat. He did as he was told and took a seat on the couch. Reign asked Jackie to walk to the truck to grab the duffel bag.

"You can't get away with killing a cop," Burke said with a chuckle. He thought that by throwing that in there, Reign would freeze up and let him go. He had stared death right in the eyes quite a few times, but what he didn't know was that he was dancing with the devil - that is, if the devil was a female.

"That's the thing. I've killed before and have been getting away with it. Just because you're a cop don't mean shit. There are cops like you who shoot unarmed black men and get away with it all of the time."

"Is this about that case with me shooting that nigger at the hospital? If it is, you're just a little too late. I go in next week to start my time. It will come to light that you are behind this and guess where you're going? Straight to where I am going. So you might as well cut me loose and let me serve my time."

"That is not enough for me. That man you shot is the love of my life. You could have taken him away from so many things - his family, his career - and it was all because of what? Because you're racist?"

"My life was in danger!" he yelled. That's what his lawyer had advised him to say if he was approached about him being a racist.

Jackie had come, and she was accompanied by a chair from the kitchen.

"That's bullshit!"

"It's not!"

"I was there when you shot him! If you felt like your life was in danger, then why didn't your partner feel the same way? I've waited for this moment since that day, and I only hoped that you would confess that you are a racist."

With strength that Burke didn't expect, Reign grabbed him by his shirt collar and forced him to sit on the chair Jackie brought into the living room. Reign passed her gun to Jackie so that she could go through the bag that Jackie had packed. She found some duct tape and began to bind his legs to the legs of the chair. She grabbed his arms and taped them at the wrists behind him.

"Make it quick and to the point," Burke stated, accepting his fate.

"Oh no. That's not how it's going to go. You don't get to have any power or control in this situation. I hold all of it," Reign said. She held her hand out towards Jackie and she reached into the bag. Jackie pulled out a ten-inch meat cleaver. She passed it to Reign and watched as the instrument in her hands caused a smile on her cousin's face.

"What is that you want from me?" Burke asked. His heart was pounding through his chest. Once he saw the cleaver come out of the bag, he knew that she was going to make him suffer before he died.

"I only want you to pay for every black man you shot - the ones that died as well as the ones who lived, including my man." Reign circled around the chair and then, without much warning, she slammed the cleaver down.

Instantly, his toes were separated from his foot. The blood-curdling scream that escaped from his mouth could be heard miles away. Jackie walked into the kitchen to get the small dish rag that she had noticed on the side of the sink.

"This little piggy went to market. This little piggy stayed home. This little piggy had roast beef. This little piggy had none," Reign said, reciting the nursery rhyme while holding his toes up. They were barely being held together by bone and muscle.

"You sick bitch!" Burke was able to yell before Reign stuffed the rag into his mouth, taping it shut.

Once she made sure that it was in there, she went after his other foot. After ripping his shirt with the cleaver, she went into the bag again and found a small torch. With another smile on her face, she ignited the torch and placed the flame against his chest. She watched as his skin melted and burned. Reign held the torch against his torso until he suffered from third degree burns. By this time, he had lost consciousness and stopped squirming.

"Okay, let's pack up and get ready to leave," Reign stated.

"What if he gets up?" Jackie asked.

"He won't. I fucked up by not having James make sure he was dead."

Reign took her gun and placed it against Burke's forehead, sending one through his thoughts. For good measure, she aimed it at his heart next and sent one through his heart, leaving a clear entrance and exit wound. Satisfied with her work, she un-taped his hands and grabbed them. Taking out her lipstick, she drew a heart on his wrist. She felt herself becoming alive again.

Reign went around the house and wiped down everything that they could have possibly touched while Jackie packed the bag. As fast as they came, they left once the deed was done.

Dropping a body always put Reign in a euphoric state and she suggested that she and Jackie went to get a drink in celebration of her being back to her old self. What she didn't know was that there was a storm brewing at the home front.

***

Senaj paced back and forth in the living room while Akuchi and Jamori watched. Reign's doctor had called Senaj to let him know that Reign had signed herself out of the hospital, but when she didn't show up at home, he started to worry. He called her nonstop, but she didn't answer. They eventually put two and two together when Jackie hadn't made it back from the store like she said she would. Akuchi began to call Jackie while Senaj called Reign.

"Y'all know the reason why they not answering, so y'all might as well stop blowing up their phones," Jamori stated.

"I know, why which is why I am. For all I know, she could be giving Christina a C-section and throwing my unborn child down a sewer," Senaj said dramatically.

"Bro, stop worrying. They've been trained to know how to handle themselves. They good," Jamori stated with a chuckle.

Senaj side-eyed Jamori and continued to pace and call Reign.

Ten minutes later, close to one in the morning, Reign and Jackie walked in, giggling like two school girls. Thy appeared to be drunk and oblivious to the three men sitting in the living room.

"Shh. We don't want to wake them up," Reign said, placing her finger against her lips and full out laughing.

Akuchi and Jamori smirked while Senaj stood there scolding them like he was their father.

Jackie turned to the living room and saw them in there. She said, "Oh shit, too late."

Reign took one look inside of the living room and saw Senaj and instantly sucked her teeth.

"Reign," he said.

"Nigga, please." Reign threw up her hand as if she was dismissing him. She headed to their bedroom and he followed right behind her, closing the door behind him.

"We need to talk."

"Yes, we do. But right now isn't good. I am past my limit of intoxication and this conversation won't be good," Reign said as she winced while taking her pants off.

"You shouldn't have left the hospital."

"And you shouldn't have cheated. But look where that has us."

"That's not fair, Reign. It was unintentional. I didn't just go out one day and decide to cheat. It happened exactly the way I told you it happened."

"How and why was her number in your phone?" Reign asked. Obviously, to her, Senaj was planning on doing something because why else would he have her number saved?

"Because - "

"I don't even want to hear it. What's done is done and that's it. I want to move past this, Senaj."

"Before we do, I need to tell you something."

"You cheated again?" Reign asked, grabbing some clothes to take a shower.

"No. Hell no. That was one mistake that definitely won't happen again. I'm pretty sure that one day you will forgive me, but - "

Reign exhaled because she really didn't want to have any conversations with Senaj. She just wanted to shower, sneak a peek at her kids, and sleep her drunkenness off. She closed her eyes before she looked over her shoulder. "Senaj, I just want to shower and kiss the kids good night. Please can we have this conversation in the morning?"

Reign began to walk away, but if Senaj didn't get this off his chest now, he felt like he would burst inside. He had a lot of time to battle himself over what he would do in the situation with Christina. His decision could possibly ruin any hope of them working out their relationship. Before Reign was fully out of the room, he blurted out, "Reign, I'm going to take custody of Christina's baby upon a DNA test proving that I am the baby's father."

Reign's heart, no matter how drunk she was, dropped to her feet. She couldn't believe what he just said to her, let alone think that this was going to work afterward. Of course, if he kept his word by giving up his rights, she would have been by his side. Her mind sped through things to say, but she was rendered speechless. She looked over her shoulder once again, causing Senaj to feel like a complete ass. The tears that cascaded down her face in warp speed spoke volumes to his heart. Hurting her was the last thing that he wanted to do, but somehow, he still managed to do so.

"You keep her child, me and mines are gone," Reign finally responded. She kept her eyes trained on him to make sure that he understood her.

From the look on her face he knew that she was serious, and it was his turn to have his heart drop to his feet.

***

The next morning, Senaj woke up with his head pounding and pain shooting up and down his back. After Reign threatened to take the kids and leave him, he decided to give Reign her space and slept on the couch. Yawning and stretching, Senaj prepared himself to get ready for his first day back to work. Although he loved Reign, he was more than happy to be away from home. He knew that if he stayed, with Reign's attitude, it would become a shit show later in the day.

He crept around the house, cautious not to wake anyone. Arriving in the room that he shared with Reign, he saw Reign sitting up in bed with her back against the headboard. She was holding Zariyah in a blanket, rocking from side to side with tears in her eyes. The moment was beautiful and Senaj wished that he had his phone to capture the moment. Senaj watched for a few more seconds until Reign looked at him and the tears fell harder.

"They let her come home too early," Reign managed to say. She was so choked up that she hiccupped in between words.

Senaj's eyebrows shot up and a mask of confusion covered his face. "She came home right on time, love. What are you talking about?" Senaj asked as he moved cautiously towards the bed.

"I woke up a half hour ago to get some water. After leaving from the kitchen, I went to go check on them and as I picked Zariyah up to place a kiss on her cheeks, she was cold. Her lips were turning blue and she looked peaceful. I didn't know what to do, so I just held her."

Senaj's heart fell to the deepest pits of his stomach. He rushed over to the bed where Reign was and grabbed Zariyah's tiny frame up and held her close. He began to check her vitals and there was a very faint pulse. Trying to stay calm, Senaj questioned, "Why didn't you come get me, Reign? How is this going to look when we get to the hospital?"

Senaj proceeded to perform CPR on Zariyah and instructed Reign to go get his brother. Reign, with tears in her eyes, ran out of the room to go wake up Akuchi. Moments later, he flew through the room with Reign and the twins on his heels.

"Come with me, bro. Drive while I continue to give my baby CPR!" Senaj yelled.

"What happened?" Jackie asked.

"Jackie and Jamori, can y'all stay with Reign until I call to let y'all know that it's okay to bring her down to the hospital?"

"Yeah, we got you, bro," Jamori answered.

"What? What the fuck you mean I gotta stay here?" Reign questioned with her arms folded across her chest.

"Right now, arguing with you is the least of my worries. Stay here like I said." The look Senaj gave Reign told her that she better had taken heed to what he had to say.

She knew that right now she wasn't his favorite person, and the way his voice boomed at his request, now wasn't the time to fuck around. Quickly placing a kiss on Zariyah's face, Reign allowed Senaj to make a dash to the car.

In the back seat of the car, as he performed CPR, he understood why Reign thought that their daughter was gone. She was cold to the touch and her lips were blue, but Senaj, being a doctor, was able to do what he needed to do to make sure that Zariyah made it.

"I can't believe her. She should have come and got me!" Senaj screamed. They were five minutes away from the hospital when NYPD pulled up behind them and flashed their lights.

"Ahh! Come on! Not right now," Akuchi growled. He continued, "Listen, I'm gonna deal with these consequences when we get to the hospital. We are too close for this nigga to stop us now."

Senaj thought on it for a quick second. He looked down at his baby girl and responded, "Bro, at this point I don't even care. Just get us there. If you get knocked for this, I got you."

"Ain't no doubt in that, bro. My main concern is my niece."

Two minutes later, they arrived at the hospital and Senaj jumped from the back seat and ran inside. Screaming for help. Akuchi was already out of the car and his hands were in the air. Two cop cars pulled in behind them and they jumped out with their guns drawn.

"Get on the ground now!" they yelled.

"Just listen! I am unarmed, my niece was having a medical emergency and she was barely breathing! I apologize for not stopping, but it was life or death and I made the decision to make sure that my niece has a chance at life!" Akuchi yelled while holding his hands in the air above his head, making his way to his knees.

A doctor came running out and stood between Akuchi and the cops, ordering them to put their guns down.

"His brother is in there asking for him. Now, I don't know what you all are going to do, but I'm taking this gentleman in and taking him to be with his family. He has done nothing wrong except do what any human would do in a situation like this. Get up, young man, and follow me," the doctor expressed.

Akuchi looked up at the doctor, who was several shades lighter than he was. In fact, he was as pale as a vampire. No one beside people of his own color helped him.

The cops were just as stunned as Akuchi and lowered their weapons. Akuchi got up from his knees and thanked God before he followed the doctor back inside of the hospital.

***

Several hours passed. Reign held K.B. against her body, trying to get him to take a nap. Several thoughts wrapped around each other as she tried to wrap her mind around what her life had turned into in the last two years. She now had two children, one of which she had cut out of the body of her best friend, who had turned snitch in a desperate way to get Reign's attention. Pearl had tried to fuck Senaj and then place the blame on him. For a moment, Reign had believed Pearl, but Nana, God rest her soul, put some things into perspective for her, and from that moment, Reign disowned Pearl. Pearl did the unthinkable and went to the police and spilled the beans on what she thought she knew about Reign being the Lipstick Killah. Reign figured that she couldn't have told the cops much because they hadn't come to knock her door down.

"Reign, Jameson has been calling your phone back to back. Let me take baby K.B. and you answer his call. It could be important," Jackie stated, coming behind Reign.

"Have you heard anything from Senaj? I don't know how I could be so stupid. Why didn't I just bring her to him?" Reign questioned. She dragged her hand across her face as she felt the stupidest she had ever felt.

"Your life isn't the same anymore, Reign, and you have to adjust to it. Sometimes things happen when you are a new parent, and it's even worse with the things that you have been through with Zariyah. Senaj has every reason to be pissed, but he is doing what he must to make sure that Zariyah is okay. Everything will be okay when Zariyah is back home."

"Jackie, I've been treating Senaj like shit lately and I can't even begin to think why. He doesn't deserve that shit, and I think if I don't fix this shit soon, I know he's going to leave me. I love that man more than my own life. Before y'all came into my life, Senaj was there for me. Even after he found out about what I do for a living. He didn't judge me or leave me, and he doesn't deserve this."

"Right now, Reign, the only thing that you have to be focused on is Zariyah and placing this phone call back to Jameson. When Senaj calls, I will let you know, but you need to get your mind off him and whether he is going to leave you or not. You know that you were strong before Senaj. Put your big girl panties on and get back to being Reign. You better get your life together and act like you know." Jackie walked out of the room.

The phone vibrated in Reign's hand and she looked at Jameson's name displayed on the screen. "Yeah," she answered.

"What's been going on with you? I know that you not backing out."

Reign dragged her fingers across her forehead. She responded, "That is definitely not the case. I'm gonna always chase the bag. There are just a few things that have been going on at the home front that needed to be taken care of. What's up? You got something new for me?"

"I wouldn't be calling if I didn't. I'm sending you a fax as we speak. This one I know you are going to like. He's been a pain in your ass and he's slowly becoming a pain in mine."

"Okay. I'll see what it is that I can do. I need a favor from you though. Being that your uncle or whoever it was that you said was captain of the NYPD, I need to know if there is a case being built against me. I have a family now and I need to be prepared if there is."

There was a brief pause before Jameson responded, "Yeah. I'll do that as soon as I can."

"Thank you."

"We'll talk soon."

With that, they hung up. Reign began to make her way to the office to grab the fax, but the phone vibrated in her hand, signaling that there was a text.

Senaj: *First, I want to let you know that Zariyah is doing okay. They have her on oxygen and so far, she is doing well. They said that she suffered from a seizure and that they are giving her meds to make sure that it doesn't happen again. Second, I want to apologize for the way I reacted. I was upset that you didn't come and get me first. It's okay for you to come down here. Have the twins bring you and baby K.B. Zariyah needs her family and I need you. Not to mention to tell you how your knuckle headed brother was about to go back to jail. LOL. I love you, Reign. And I love our family. Let's get this shit together, babe.*

A smile came across Reign's face and after a simple "I love you too" response, Reign went to grab her papers from the fax machine and then told the twins to get ready. She grabbed K.B. and got dressed. Her heart fluttered as she thought about Senaj's words. He was right. It was time for their family to get back on track.

Chapter Four

Rasheed and Polite sat at the bar at Smalls Jazz Club. They each had a beer sitting in front of them. Although they were there, they weren't enjoying themselves. Oddly enough, they missed their best friend Senaj. Nothing had gone down between them, but with Senaj being with Reign, and them knowing what she did for a living, it pushed them away. They weren't scared of what she did. They just couldn't understand why she did it. They didn't want to be associated with it. It had been years since they had gotten their noses dirty and they would like it to remain that way.

"Man, this is some bullshit. Senaj has always been my nigga and I miss him. Whose choice was it for us not to hang with him?" Polite expressed, slurring a little.

"It's not about him. It's about his girl. We already know too much and we not a part of that life any more. I don't know about you, but I don't want to have to go down for some shit that ain't got nothing to do with me."

"So we can't hang with our boy because of that?"

Rasheed looked over towards Polite and chuckled. "We could hang with him, but for our sake, we need to let him know that anything that he has to say about his girl, we don't need to know. Send him a text and see if he wants to have a few drinks. I'll be back. I gotta take a leak."

He got up from his seat and patted Polite's shoulder with a smile on his face, but it quickly disappeared. He made his way to the bathroom and walked over to a urinal to release himself. His back was to the door, but he heard the door open and close anyway.

"Why haven't you been answering my calls?" a female voice said.

"I've been busy. What are you doing here?" Rasheed asked. He shook his dick and placed it back into his jeans and then walked over to the sink to wash his hands.

"Because you haven't been answering my phone calls. I've done what you asked of me, but I don't think that it's going to work. He's in love with her and they have a baby together. Plus, it's all gonna go to shit when Senaj decides to get a DNA test and finds out that this isn't his baby. Rasheed, you know that there is a fifty percent chance that this is your baby."

"Christina, I know for a fact that the baby that you are carrying is not mine. Remember, we've been using condoms," Rasheed responded as he leaned against the sink.

"Look, I don't know what more it is you want me to do. You know that once Reign finds out about any of this, she's going to make sure that none of us is about to live to tell about it."

"Reign isn't the only one that knows some things. And if I must, I will go back to my old ways. Do what you have to do, and everything will be fine."

Christina didn't know that the fuck she was doing. A month before she had sex with Senaj, she had sex with Rasheed. Granted, they did use a condom, but it was a condom that she provided. The condom had tiny holes in it because Christina's plan was to get pregnant by Rasheed and still have a way to possibly see Senaj. She didn't want no smoke with Reign, but she did the fucked-up thing by sleeping with Senaj, knowing that Reign would have an issue. Christina knew that Rasheed was the father and she no longer wanted to be a part of Rasheed's plan.

"Okay, Rasheed. We have until the baby is born. I'm telling you, Senaj is going to want a DNA test done and if not him, then Reign will. I'll play your game for now."

Rasheed began to move toward the door to go back to Polite, but Christina moved into his path. She looked at Rasheed with hunger in her eyes. They had sexed a few times. Christina knew exactly what he was working with, and she wanted it.

"Christina, you know damn well that we can't get into that right now. Polite is out there waiting on me and if I take too long, he gonna come in here looking for me. Why don't you go home, shower, and cozy up with your son or something? When I'm done here, I'll stop by and give you what you want," Rasheed responded while dragging his thumb across her chin.

Christina pouted but nonetheless agreed to what Rasheed said. She'd rather get dicked down in the comforts of her own home than in a dirty men's bathroom any day. Christina gathered herself together and left the bathroom, making her way home.

Rasheed walked to the sink and turned on the nozzle for the cold water. Slightly bending, Rasheed gathered water into his hands and splashed his face. He looked at himself in the mirror as he thought about what he was doing behind Senaj's back. It was selfish but, in his mind, he was doing what was right.

Hearing the door to the bathroom open, Rasheed looked in the mirror and saw Polite standing at the entrance.

"Nigga, what the fuck is taking so long? Senaj can't make it. Let's go get fucked up. There are some fine-ass bitches that just walked in here," Polite spoke with a slur.

Rasheed placed a smile on his face and walked out of the bathroom behind Polite.

*****

The last place Reign wanted to be was at the hospital. Her heart was aching as she sat next to her daughter's bed, dressed in a sterile gown, mask, head cap, and protective covers for her shoes. The tears wouldn't stop as she watched Zariyah's chest rise and fall. Senaj was on the opposite side of the bed and his head hung low. The twins and Akuchi were in the waiting room giving the couple some alone time with their child. Darkness had easily crept in and there was a disgusting storm coming their way. Thunder cracked and lightning etched across the sky.

"We need to talk," Reign said, breaking the silence.

Senaj sat up in his seat and dragged his hand down his face. He blinked a few times and responded, "Yes, I know."

"I don't know what happened. Everything seemed like it was going so good and things just went downhill. I just want the old us back," Reign responded. *What is up with all of these tears? I have never cried so much in my damn life.*

Senaj moved his way to Reign and grabbed her into a hug. After smelling her hair, he kissed the top of her head and sighed. "It's not up to us to figure out where we went wrong. It's up to us to figure out how to get back on track. Let's move to a new place, get rid of our old ones, and start a new life. Give up the whole assassin thing and let me take care of our family."

Skkkuuurrrt! Wait a minute? Did he just tell me to stop doing what I do to make money? Did he just tell me to give up the only thing I know how to do? She coached herself to calm down because now was not the time to act a plumb fool. Reign was going to do something that she had never done before and that was to submit to her man. She decided that she would think about what it was that he was asking - at least for the time being. She'd deal with repercussions later. After all, she was working with Jameson and she couldn't renege on their agreement.

"Okay, Senaj. I agree. It is time for me to hang my guns up and buckle down and take care of my family while you bring home the bacon," Reign managed to choke out. She didn't like the way it rolled off her tongue and felt her throat moisten as if the bile from her stomach was threatening to make its way up.

Senaj pushed Reign back at the shoulders and looked at her in disbelief. *That was too easy*, he thought. He watched as she placed a smile on her face. With one appearing on his face, he asked, "I feel like you're up to something, but I'm not quite sure. But I'll leave it alone for now. You want to go and get the twins and Akuchi? Or shall I?"

"I'll go get them. You stay with Zariyah," Reign responded as she looked down at Zariyah. Senaj saw her eyes misting over and then she quickly wiped the tears away. Reign hesitantly turned around and walked out of the room.

The knot that was forming in her throat threatened to surface as she walked down the hallway. She was fighting to make sure that she didn't break down right the middle of the hospital.

When she made it to the waiting area, everyone rushed over to her, firing off questions about Zariyah.

"They said that it was a seizure. They are going to keep her until tomorrow for observations and then hopefully, by the grace of God, we can bring her home," Reign blurted out to cut them off, simply answering their questions with that one answer.

"Can we see her?" Jamori asked.

"Yes, but make sure y'all stop at the nurses' station to grab some of the sterile gear. Jackie, I need to talk to you for a moment."

Akuchi and Jamori looked at Reign and Jackie with raised eyebrows and then hesitantly walked away.

"What's up, cuz?" Jackie asked. She knew, but the look in Reign's eyes said that there was something seriously bothering her.

Reign snatched off the sterile gown and sat on the chair that Jamori had previously occupied and leaned back with her head against the wall.

"My dumb ass just agreed with Senaj that I would put my guns away and become 'domestic'. Fuck would I go and do that for? Don't get me wrong, but this is literally my job. It's a fucked-up job but it's how I make my money. Plus, I need to finish this contract with Jameson. Cuz, I'm stressed. I need a blunt and a drink as soon as possible."

"Shut up. You don't even smoke no more. Just explain to Senaj that you will finish what you have to do with Jameson."

"If only it was that easy."

"Trust me, Senaj would hear you out."

Reign exhaled because she knew that it would be impossible. When Senaj was serious, that was the bottom line.

Reign stood up and took the fax sheet that she had received before going to the hospital. Jameson had come through with information on Pablo's son. Pablo was a man that she had been at war with because she had killed one of his men. Reign, Senaj, and her ex-best friend were out having dinner when Pablo rolled up and began to air shit out. Reign had signaled for Senaj to get Pearl out of the restaurant, since she was pregnant with Kahlil at the time. She had exchanged gunfire and at the end, she was the victor.

On the paper was a picture of Pablo's son, Juan. Juan had showed up to her home and shot up the front of her house, seeking revenge, killing her Nana in the process. Since then, he had disappeared. On the paper there was an address for where he was at. He was laying low in Philadelphia.

"What's that?" Jackie asked.

"Something from Jameson." Reign tucked the paper into her pocket.

Jackie side-eyed Reign and bit her tongue to keep herself from asking any further questions. She grabbed Reign's hand and they moved to Zariyah's room. Zariyah's eyes were open and looking around the room and everyone was in awe at how alert she was. No one could deny the smiles on their faces were as big as the sun.

Reign's heart swelled. Her baby girl was going to be okay and nothing else mattered - at least for that moment.

Mimi

Chapter Five

The snow fell from the dark sky in thick blankets. Fall had been quickly replaced by winter in late November. Juan was bundled up nice and warm in his North Face coat and construction Timberland boots. His plan for that day wasn't to leave his small apartment for a damn thing, but without realizing it, he had used all his Backwoods and needed to make a run to get some. Luckily for him, the snow had just began to fall and he didn't have to worry about digging his car out.

The ride to the local Wawa on Arch Street was a short but slippery one. Upon entering the store, Juan went straight to the kiosk so that he could order a sandwich. He wasn't hungry, but he knew once he got high, he would be. He took his time in ordering a buffalo chicken sub with lettuce, mayonnaise, banana peppers, and extra buffalo sauce. He went into one of the beverage freezers, grabbed a Pepsi, and headed to the counter. He was not one to eavesdrop, but he couldn't help it when he heard a female slightly arguing into the phone.

"This isn't right. You made me come all the way from New York City to come see you and you are leaving me stranded because your baby mother decided to come over? Kick the bitch out and come and get me! The bus? It's almost one in the morning, I took the last bus out here, what you mean?" The girl's voice escalated.

He couldn't help but turn his attention to her. Her hips poking out from under her fitted North Face is what caught his attention first. Black gloves covered her hands and construction Timberlands were on her feet as well. Juan didn't usually find women outside of his race attractive, but this woman who stood before him was a black goddess and he couldn't help but to be drawn to her. The black women he was used to seeing had fake everything and he liked his women natural. Her natural curves, no makeup, real lashes, and even her hair, which sat in a ponytail, her curls kinky and tight, stirred something in his body. Her light-colored eyes glistened under the light and misted over just a tad bit.

Juan knew that he should mind his business, but he couldn't. He was drawn to her like a moth to a flame. He sucked his teeth to himself and slowly walked in her direction. She was swiftly cursing dude out but abruptly stopped when she noticed that Juan was looking at her.

"Can I help you?" she asked with much attitude.

Juan shook his head as if he was shaking the fog from his brain. For a split second he asked himself what he was thinking and even thought about going back to wait for his food. Instead, his mouth opened and he began talking. He said, "I'm sorry. I wasn't trying to listen to your conversation, but I just had to let you know how beautiful you are, and you don't need to be arguing with a fuck boy."

A smirk appeared on her face. It quickly faded when she realized that she was still on the phone because as the person began to speak, her grimace returned. She said, "You don't need to worry who the hell I'm talking to because you left me stranded. For all this shit, I could have stayed home. You know damn well that I didn't have the bread to come out here. You know what? Fuck you!"

"Damn!" Juan managed to say.

"I'm sorry about that," she apologized and pointed her head to the floor.

"You don't have to apologize on behalf of some dude. By what I caught from your conversation, he ain't shit."

"Buffalo chicken sub!" the clerk called out.

Juan walked up to the counter and paid for his sub and some more Backwoods. He peeped the girl looking at him and he couldn't bring it upon himself to just leave her just standing there. He also didn't want anyone to think that he was some type of creep.

With his bag in hand, he approached her yet again. He said, "Look, I don't think that it would be a good idea for you to be roaming these streets at night. I have an apartment not too far from here where you will be able to get some proper rest, eat, and be warm."

"I don't know you," she said defensively.

"I can assure you that being a creep isn't on my agenda. I know we don't know each other, but I would feel better if I knew that you were safe instead of out here in these streets where you know no one."

"What is your name?"

"Juan. You?" he asked as he reached his hand out for her to shake.

"The only way that I will feel comfortable going with you is if you write down your full name, address, and what you drive down on a piece of paper and give it to the lady clerk."

Juan nodded his head and without hesitation he did what was asked. This new girl he met was peering over his shoulder and typing on her phone. He was pretty sure that she was sending a message to a few of her peoples for just in case purposes. Juan had no intentions of hurting her. From his heart, he just wanted to make sure that she was safe. He could only hope that if he had a sister that someone would do the same for her and would make sure that she was safe.

"I never got your name," Juan said as they climbed into the car.

She smiled and said, "Jazmine."

Juan smiled back at Jazmine and continued the short distance to his apartment. When they reached his apartment, at the door, they took off their coats and shoes. Juan told Jazmine to get comfortable on the couch while he poured them something to drink.

Jazmine did what she was told but she couldn't help but to feel nervous. She knew better than going with a stranger to their house. This was new territory for her and she knew no one in the whole state of Pennsylvania besides her "boyfriend", who had put his baby mother before her. This was how some people went missing. But what was she supposed to do? She was stranded and didn't have enough money to get a hotel room for the night and make it home the next day. That was the reason why she went against her better judgement and went with Juan.

"Here you go," Juan stated, passing Jazmine a closed bottle of water, and then he sat next to her.

She was grateful that it was closed and not inside of a cup. Juan sat next to her and rolled up his much needed blunt and watched MSNBC's *Lockup.*

"I don't usually go with strangers -"

"You don't have to explain yourself. I can assure you that I am not a creep and that I am only making sure that you have a warm place to stay. It's cold out there, and you don't need to be out there stranded. If you would like, in the morning I could take you to the bus station so you can get on the bus and head back to New York."

A smile formed on her face and she said, "I can't thank you enough."

"Don't worry about it. You burn?"

"Hell yeah," she answered.

They sat together on the couch and smoked and talked about nothing. Juan listened to her as she explained that she had been with her boyfriend for three years. He was from New York, but his mother decided to move to Philly and he was sixteen at the time, so he had no choice but to go with her. His first year in Philly he ended up getting a girl pregnant. She was heartbroken. She was completely faithful to him and he had hurt her to the core. Like a dummy, she forgave him because he told her that it was a one-time thing, that he was out with some friends and it was an accident. She believed him, but most times when she would want to come visit, his baby mother would pop up and he would cancel. Like this night. He knew that she was on her way. He knew that she wouldn't have a way to get back to New York, but he still cancelled on her.

"You know where he lives? 'Cause we could go over there and see what is really going on. To me it sounds like he's still messing with her. If it was a one-time thing, he shouldn't have to cancel on you if you're his woman," Juan said. He felt bad for her. He was a lover boy and if he couldn't commit fully to a female, he'd rather stay single until he was ready.

Jazmine shook her head slowly. The tears that she had been holding back while talking to Juan began to spill from her eyes. He was attentive to her and she didn't even know him. She wiped her tears and said, "I couldn't let you do that. I appreciate it, but I know if I go over there it's gonna be some mess and I don't want you to get wrapped up in my bullshit."

"I insist," Juan simply responded. He smiled again, making Jazmine feel warm inside. He continued, "Go in the bathroom and wash your face. There are fresh wash cloths in the closet next to the bathroom. You need answers and of course he won't be expecting you so if he is up to something, he will be in complete shock. I got your back."

Jazmine took one second to think about it. She decided that she did want to go. She needed to see his infidelity in her face because she knew if she left Philly without seeing it, she would continue to fuck with him. She loved him, but her love had a limit.

She stood from the couch and walked towards the bathroom. The weed they had smoked had her on cloud nine and feeling mighty fine. She walked inside the bathroom, her hand caressing the wall, checking for a light switch. There wasn't a light switch, but she did feel what she thought was a leather covered body part. Instinctively she opened her mouth to scream, but a rag was placed over her face and an arm wrapped around her neck, tight enough to stop her from trying to escape. She panicked and wondered what she had done to deserve this.

"I won't kill you. I just need you out of my way," a female voice said.

Her eyes popped opened at the husky, feminine voice. She tried to fight against her, figuring that because she was a female, it would be easy. Jazmine realized that she was no match, that this woman could have very well been She-Hulk. Minutes passed by as she felt her fight getting weak. She tried her hardest to fight, but her eyes had gotten too heavy and her muscles relaxed. Things faded to black and she was in dream land.

Juan sat on the couch rolling up another blunt to smoke on their way to this dummy mission. Hearing Jazmine's footsteps, he said, "Took you long enough. I thought you were making the washcloths back there."

Juan's laughter echoed through the room but quickly stopped when a blacked-out ringed throwing dagger lodged itself into his thigh flesh. Seconds later there was another dagger thrown and lodged in his arm.

"Ahhh! What the fuck?" he yelled. He looked in the direction where Jazmine had disappeared and noticed a completely different female. In fact, it was his worst nightmare. His eyes ballooned at the sight of Reign and immediately he tried to remove the daggers from his arm and thigh. He was barely able to move.

Reign walked over to Juan, who now had slid from the couch and onto the floor. Her daggers were dipped in very potent Black Mamba venom and he was slowly becoming paralyzed. She needed to act fast or the words she wanted to tell him wouldn't matter. He would soon be dead. Reign stood over Juan and looked him in his eyes. The horror was written in his eyes.

"Oh, you thought that I wasn't going to catch up with you, right?" Reign asked with a sickening laugh. She answered herself, "Nah, you thought you was going to pick up and move to a different state, possibly bounce around in different states. But the first thing you did was go an hour and some odd minutes out of the city. You must be stupid - obviously, because I caught up with you. Anyway, let me talk fast because you only have a few more minutes before you die."

Reign took her daggers out of his arm and thigh. Using a towel she had tucked in her back pocket, she wiped the blood off the knives, threw the rag on top of him and placed the daggers inside the holsters strapped to her thighs. She continued to talk. "You would have probably had a chance of living if you had not come to my house and shot it up. My Nana was in the house and you know what? She is no longer with me because of you. If the beef would have just stayed between us, you wouldn't have been in this position. Your father deserved to die. My Nana didn't."

"W-w-where i-i-is J-J-Jazmine?" Juan asked.

"Who? Oh, shorty that was in the bathroom? She doesn't have nothing to do with this beef. What you didn't know was ole girl at the gas station was my eyes and ears and dropped me the information that I was going to need. In fact, she has been for about two weeks and let me know that you frequent that Wawa's often. Well, that's neither here nor there. Your death has nothing to do with you seeking revenge for your dad but for the simple fact I lost my father's mother!" Reign held back her tears because she knew her Nana was smiling down on her.

Reaching into the side of her bootie, she retrieved her Christian Louboutin lipstick and examined his wrist. His eyes had sadness in them but there was nothing that Reign could do other than draw her signature heart onto his wrist while Juan's bodily fluids began to leak from his body. The foul stench of human waste lingered in the air as Reign looked down at Juan's body. She needed to see him take his last breath before she made her way back home to her family in New York.

Reign was leaning against the door frame when she noticed Juan's eyes becoming heavy. His body was stiff, and her stomach was damn near turning in knots as she had no choice but to inhale the stench of the shit that she was sure was smushed against his ass. The gasp that she heard as he took his last breath sent her adrenaline rushing. With a satisfied smile, she used her gloved hand to turn the knob on the door and got ready to flee, but the screaming of the female that she had knocked out with chloroform jolted her body to stiffness. She turned back around and shut the door. Jazmine was standing in the doorway of the living room from the direction of the bathroom and screaming. She couldn't take her eyes from Juan's dead cold eyes.

"What did you do?" Jazmine yelled.

"I don't want to do nothing to you. My beef wasn't with you, so I suggest you cut all that yelling out because I promise you, it could get really ugly for you real fast," Reign threatened.

"What the fuck?"

"Listen to me and listen to me good, I'm walking out of here and you gonna forget that you even saw me. I'm going against what I believe in. You're a witness and I'm allowing you to live. Now, like I said, you need to shut your mouth."

"I've already called the police."

Reign rolled her eyes. This girl was innocent, and she didn't want to have to slump her, but she said five words that Reign didn't want to hear so Reign did what she had to do. She pulled out her Rose Gold Maxim 9, and one bullet to Jazmine's head silenced her.

Reign heard the sirens of Philadelphia Police Department off in the distance. She had no time to place her signature lipstick-drawn heart on Jazmine. Besides, she was just a casualty.

Sucking her teeth, Reign ran from the apartment and down the stairs. She was out of the building in less than a minute and racing down the block to climb inside her rented Denali. As she busted a U-turn, she took the shades that she had shielding her eyes off and watched as the police came flying from the opposite direction. She made the right at the corner and proceeded to follow the GPS directions for getting on the highway to head back home.

Mimi

Chapter Six

Christina woke up to the sun shining brightly on her face and her son, My'Heir, cuddled up against her growing belly. Not even five seconds later she was jumping out of the bed and giving the toilet some face time. The burn from the bile burned her throat as she threw up the little contents of her stomach into the toilet. Tears etched the corners of her eyes, not because of emotion, but because she had squeezed her eyes shut so tight they leaked out. When she was done, she leaned her back against the wall, trying to regain her composure. This was not a part of her game plan when she had decided to show up out of blue. Sure, she was gonna try to reconnect with Senaj, but she wasn't supposed to end up pregnant again. The fact that Rasheed, Senaj's best friend, was using her to stop Senaj from messing with Reign was now ringing in her brain that this plan was ridiculous. She was pregnant with her second child and she was sure as the sky was blue that it was Rasheed's and not Senaj's. Rasheed being the hard-headed person he was didn't want to believe that it was his baby. Christina would prove it one way or another.

Christina stood up from the floor and looked at herself. Her eyes had rings around them and the bags that were hanging from her eyes told her that she needed sleep. Something longer than four hours. Reaching for her wash rag, she wet it with cold water and placed it against her face and neck. The room spun as she tried to hold herself steady against the bathroom sink. This was the part of pregnancy that she didn't like. She could deal with anything else, but the morning sickness had to go. Finally, moments later, Christina was beginning to feel better and she walked inside her room to wake her son up to get him ready for daycare.

The telephone ringing - her house phone, which rarely rang - caught her by surprise. My'Heir was now awake, so she walked out of the room to answer. The caller on the other end was impatient and was ready to hang up until he heard her voice on the other end. Christina knew who it was without looking at the caller ID.

"Hello," she spoke with irritation lacing her voice.

"Well good morning to you too," Rasheed said into the receiver.

"It's not so good. What do you want, Rasheed?"

"I need you to go see Senaj today."

"What?" Christina asked. When she woke up that morning she vowed to be done with whatever plan Rasheed had come up with. With a new baby on the way, she wanted to focus on that.

"Don't turn deaf now, baby girl."

"Rasheed." Christina sighed.

"Don't tell me that you are having second thoughts."

That was exactly what Christina was having. She didn't want to be his pawn anymore. Christina pinched the bridge of her nose, feeling a headache coming on. She expressed, "Listen, Rasheed. I don't know why you have this need to try and break up Senaj and Reign, but I don't want no parts of this. So many people are going to be hurt behind this and frankly, I'm not trying to be in Reign's way when shit hit the fan. That woman is bat shit crazy over Senaj and Senaj right now isn't in no position to be trying to start another family with someone who's not even carrying his baby."

"How do you know that it's not his baby? We've used condoms."

"Remember that day when we first had sex? That was what, two days before Senaj texted me thinking that he was texting Reign? We didn't use a condom that night. You were so drunk off your ass you don't remember that. But I damn sure do because you know why? I was as sober as sober can be and when I told you to put on a condom, you used the lame ass excuse that you were allergic to latex. My dumb ass should have known better, but I didn't and now look. My dumb ass is pregnant with your baby. Whatever infatuation that you have with Senaj and Reign, you need to handle that yourself. He's your best friend so you let him know how you feel about Reign. I doubt that he would leave her, being that she done had his child, but Senaj being who is, will listen to what you have to say."

Rasheed chuckled on the other end of the phone. "That latex thing does sound like some shit that I would say. We still not sure that the baby is mine."

"You want me to prove it? I'm far enough along to have the doctor do a non-evasive paternity test. I knew from the beginning that you would deny that you could be the father. I will call and make the appointment. You just show up. Oh, and I'm gonna do you one better. I'm gonna not only pay for it, but I'm going to pay to have the results rushed, just so that I can prove it to you."

Christina couldn't tell, but on the other end of the phone, reality was hitting Rasheed. He didn't want a baby let alone with Christina. His stomach twisted at the thought and all he wanted to do was throw his breakfast back up. He finally spoke, "Just let me know when and where. And if this baby isn't mine, you continue to do as I say. Do you understand?"

"Let me tell you something and you need to understand this. That will not happen. I'm not getting in between them two, even if it is Senaj's baby. I regret coming back here and running into you. I will pack my things and move me, My'Heir, and the new baby far, far, far away from here."

"And what if it's mine? You think you just gonna take my baby away?"

"Nope. Whether you want to be here for the baby or not, the courts will deal with that and make you."

Rasheed cut her off and said, "But you would pick up and leave if it was Senaj's baby, not even giving him that option? What the fuck is it about that nigga?"

"Unlike him, you don't have a crazy girlfriend. I don't know what she is entirely capable of doing. I only know what you told me and how can I even take your word for it. I have come to see that you are jealous of Senaj and that could be the only reason as to why you are going through such lengths. I have to go. You need to re-evaluate your life and leave Senaj alone and let him live his life."

Christina was done with the conversation. She had to get her son ready and didn't have any more minutes to put up with Rasheed's mess. In fact, she had half a mind to go ahead and speak with Reign and Senaj about Rasheed. *Maybe that's just what I'll do*, she thought as she got herself and her son dressed.

***

"Aye yo, y'all know where the iron at?" Jamori asked Jackie and Akuchi, who were sitting together on the sofa watching an old Steven Segal movie.

"No. Senaj was the last one with it. He used it before he left to go to work this morning," Akuchi spoke, not taking his eyes from the TV.

"Wait. What you need the iron for?" Jackie asked, looking at him. Jamori was dressed in just dress pants and dress shoes. He was holding a white button-down dress shirt in his hands. Jackie continued, "Where are you going?"

"Why do you always have to be so nosy?"

"Because you are sneaky, and if I don't ask, I don't know. And with all the shit this family has been going through, I need to know what everybody is up to." Jackie was now standing with her hands on her hips.

"If you must know, I have a date."

"A date?"

"Yes, a date. Now if you don't mind, I need to go and iron my shirt."

Jamori left the living room and made his way into the room that Senaj and Reign shared. There were boxes all over the place due to them moving soon. The twins and Akuchi didn't like it, but they understood that they were now a family of four and needed the space. Zariyah and K.B. began crying, which called for both Akuchi and Jackie to get up from the movie to go change them and feed them. K.B. was a few months shy of turning one and Zariyah was quickly approaching three months. Jackie grabbed Zariyah while Akuchi grabbed K.B.

Reign was walking inside of the house just as Jackie finished warming Zariyah's bottle and Akuchi was mixing some baby cereal with baby food for K.B.

"What's up, y'all?" Reign asked, making her way to the bathroom so that she could wash her hands and then to her bedroom to change into a clean tank top. It was cold out, but it was warm enough in the house for her to rock the tank. Reign went back into the living room, took Zariyah out of Jackie's hands, and placed kisses on Zariyah's face. She had to get up early to go meet with Jameson to collect her money from her last job, which was Juan.

"You're 'bout to get her all riled up after she eats, Reign," Jackie stated.

Reign rolled her eyes and shrugged her shoulders, not caring. She had missed her babies this morning. K.B. was about to be next too and he would be super turnt. He was older than Zariyah, so he would be lit for a little bit longer than Zariyah.

"I don't know why you always say something. She gonna get them all riled up and take they asses in the room for another nap with her on that big-ass bed of hers." Akuchi chuckled.

"Nah. No naps today. I have to go back out with Senaj. I wish they were old enough so that I could bring them outside to play in the snow. It's so beautiful outside."

"Akuchi, baby, we need to get a life. Everybody around us is going out except us," Jackie pouted.

"Who's everybody? It's just me and Senaj."

Akuchi interrupted and said, "Nope. Jamori in there getting ready for a date."

Reign's eyes popped out of her as she almost screamed in Zariyah's ear. It was a shock for Jamori to be going out on a date. Since they had gotten to New York from Florida, he had only put in some work with Reign and mostly stayed in the house with his baby cousin and baby brother.

"You lyin'?" Reign stated, more shocked than they were.

"No shit. He in there ironing his clothes and everything," Jackie stated.

"Oh, I have got to see this."

"Where are you and Senaj going?" Jackie asked. She took a seat on the accent chair that sat next to the couch by Akuchi.

"I don't even want to talk about it. Let me get through it first and I'll tell you all about it when it's done and over with."

Jackie understood. She sat back and watched the movie and decided that she would no longer be the babysitter. She needed to be out and having fun with Akuchi. It seemed like all they did was watch the kids, and while that wasn't a problem for her, she just knew that she should be out somewhere shaking her ass on her man's dick in somebody's club.

Reign had taken over where Akuchi and Jackie had left off and sat with both Zariyah and Kahlil on her lap. Ten minutes passed and out walked Jamori, dressed in slacks, button-up crispy white shirt, and a blazer that matched his pants. All eyes were tuned to him and he felt vulnerable.

"What y'all motherfuckers looking at?" he asked as he checked himself in the mirror that was on the wall by the door.

"Fuck what we looking at, who the fuck you going out with? You been up here for almost a year and you ain't never had no bitch around us. So, who is she?" Reign asked. She was serious about wanting to know who the bitch was, especially if it had to deal with her baby cousin.

"I'm not telling y'all so y'all can scare her away. Nope!"

"Jamori, stop it. You know us better than that. We would just like to meet her," Jackie said with a smirk on her face.

"That look on your face is the exact reason why I won't. I'll be back later. If y'all need me, call me."

Jamori placed his keys and wallet in his pocket and left the house.

Reign was going to make it her business one way or another to find out who the girl was. For now, she would leave it alone. Her life with her man and kids is what needed her attention, and that's what she is going to focus on – not to mention that meeting with Senaj was making her nervous. All that she knew was that he wanted to meet with her so they could talk. With everything that had been going on, she had every reason to worry.

"Akuchi, have you spoken to your parents?" Reign asked as she put a sleeping Zariyah in the portable playpen. Kahlil was crawling around on the floor, playing with a few plastic blocks.

"Actually, I haven't. Why, what's up?" he asked, facing Reign. Jackie had slid off into the kitchen for a quick bite to eat.

"Senaj told me about the exchange between your mom and him and I think that I need to speak with y'all mom in order to set things straight."

Akuchi exhaled because he didn't want to go down this lane - at least not without Senaj in their presence. He was the one who mouthed off to their mother. Akuchi said, "I don't think it's you who need to do the talking with my mom. It's Senaj who disrespected my mother."

"Disrespected? How is that possible when he was only defending his child and his child's mother?" Reign didn't understand. Senaj was being a man about the situation.

"You weren't there, Reign. It wasn't what he said. It was the tone that he took with Mother that's where the disrespect came from. Where we are from, you don't do that. He didn't have to agree with anything that she was saying, but he could have said some things differently."

"I understand. Do you think you could get your parents to come back up here? I would like for them to meet the kids. Get your mom and Senaj talking again. I never got the chance to know my mom and the memories that I have of her are faint. I don't know how long of a grudge your mom and Senaj can hold, but I can tell that I don't need anything to happen to either one of them while they are mad at each other," Reign explained.

Akuchi nodded his head and responded, "I can see what I can do. But I can't make any promises."

"That's all that I could ask for. One more thing. You mind watching - "

"I don't mind. I know you have to go meet with Senaj," Akuchi stated.

Jackie came switching out of the kitchen just in the nick of time. She heard their conversation and was boiling inside that Akuchi would agree to watch the kids yet again.

"You do know that we have a life of our own," Jackie spit.

Reign stopped in her tracks. She was on her way up the stairs to go take a shower and get ready to meet Senaj. "Yes, I know," Reign responded, twisting her body towards Jackie with her hand on her hip.

"Then you should know that Akuchi and I have plans."

"We do?" Akuchi asked, confused.

"Y'all do? Because he just said that he didn't mind watching the kids for me."

"Well, that's because I had a surprise for us. Sorry, Reign, but we can't babysit today."

Reign looked back and forth between Akuchi and Jackie before she nodded her head. She asked them if they could at least get them dressed while she took a quick shower to get ready. They agreed, but they noticed the attitude written on Reign's face. She knew this time would come, but she didn't expect for it to come this soon. Before climbing into the shower, she sent Senaj a text letting him know that she would be at the restaurant with the kids.

After her shower, she moisturized her skin with Palmer's cocoa butter lotion. No matter what other lotions Reign used, she would always go back to using Palmer's. She loved not only the smell, but how it left her skin feeling smooth. Reign dressed in simple jogging pants, a short sleeve V-neck shirt, and the jacket that went with the joggers. On her feet she wore her black suede Timb's and placed her hair in a simple pony-tail. She grabbed her coat and made it downstairs. Jackie was just placing Zariyah in her snowsuit and strapping her into her car seat.

"I'll help you bring them outside," Akuchi spoke as he lifted Zariyah and her car seat.

Reign walked over to the couch and hoisted Kahlil onto her waist and followed Akuchi out.

"What is Jackie's problem?" Reign asked once they were near the car, securing the kids in.

"What do you mean?"

"Her attitude and the way she said that y'all had plans."

Akuchi chuckled and responded, "You're reading way too much into it. She didn't have an attitude."

Reign placed her hands on her hips and gave Akuchi a knowing look. She thought about her rebuttal, but decided against it. She finished helping Akuchi lock the kids into the car. She gave Akuchi a hug and climbed inside the car. She drove to Peaches, located on Lewis Avenue in Brooklyn. When she arrived, Senaj was waiting outside talking on his cell phone. When he noticed her, he disconnected his call and made his way to the car.

"Hey, babe," Senaj said, leaning in for a kiss.

"Grab the stroller from the trunk," Reign returned after placing a kiss on his lips.

Senaj grabbed the stroller and unfolded it and proceeded to help Reign get out of the car.

"I need to tell you something, but I'll wait until we are in the restaurant," Senaj spoke.

Reign looked at him to read his expression. All she got was worry, and she couldn't help but to begin to worry too.

"You take them inside and I'll be right in."

Reign closed the trunk and watched Senaj walk into Peaches. Shaking off the bad feeling that was coursing through her body, she closed the car doors and followed Senaj into Peaches. He was already seated and was removing

Kahlil's coat. Zariyah was already out of her snow suit and laying on top of it, sleeping peacefully.

"What is it that you have to talk to me about?"

Senaj paused and thought about his words before he spoke. Christina had found out a way to contact him and asked him if he and Reign could meet with her. Of course, because of the situation she had caused, he was kind of skeptical. Christina assured him that it would be best if they did meet with her, so he agreed.

"Before I tell you anything, just make sure to keep an open mind and that this could be important."

Reign squinted her eyes and looked at Senaj. With skepticism, she responded, "Okay, well, don't keep me in suspense."

"Christina called me and - "

Reign cut him off and said, "Hold up. You got some fucking nerve."

"Would you let me finish before you jump ship? I asked you to keep an open mind."

"When it comes to that bitch, I will never have an open mind."

Senaj sighed and sat back in his seat. His next words needed to be the right ones. He said, "I know Christina is a sore subject, but it didn't sound like she was on some fuck shit."

"Says the nigga who had his whole dick up in her. And got her pregnant. I can't believe I brought these kids out in this weather for this bullshit."

There was the sound of the door opening, and a cold burst of air engulfed the inside of Peaches. Christina came walking in with a very pregnant belly and her son clinging to her left hand. She looked around the room and a small smile formed on her face. She began walking towards them and almost got the nerve to turn back around when she saw the glare on

Reign's face. Christina knew she couldn't keep quiet about Rasheed, so she pressed on. Upon arriving at the table, she felt the tension.

"Hey y'all," she said as she approached.

"Hey y'all is a greeting amongst friends, and as far as I know ain't none of us friends at this table. Sit down and let's make this quick," Reign spat.

Senaj side-eyed Reign, who in return rolled her eyes.

Christina snapped her mouth shut and proceeded to take My'Heir's coat off and place him inside the high chair that the restaurant provided. Once he was situated, she did the same for herself. A waiter came over and took their orders. Reign and Senaj ordered baked mac and cheese, yams, and fried chicken while Christina ordered the same and added collard greens and cornbread. She was eating for two and had to feed her son from her plate.

"Okay, first of all, let me apologize for the shit that I caused. I had no right to do so when I know what I know. This had gone far enough. I know I disrupted y'all household, and that is not who I am as a person today," Christina began.

"Spit it out already," Reign said and sipped her peach mango iced tea from a straw.

"Reign." Senaj sighed.

"Reign my ass. It's because of you that we are in this mess."

"Would you just listen to her?"

"She has the floor and she's taking forever to say what she has to say."

"I'm trying to get to that. Please just allow me to do so," Christina jumped in. She was far from a punk and she knew what part she played in this, but she refused to sit down and allow Reign to treat her as such. When neither Reign nor Senaj said anything, she continued, "The only reason why I said that

Senaj was the father of my baby is because Rasheed asked me to do so."

Both Reign and Senaj looked at each other, shocked by what she said. They looked at each other, but Reign was the one who spoke, "Please elaborate, because I'm confused as to why his best friend would ask you to do such a thing."

Everything in Christina told her to stop while she was ahead but she knew to stop this bullshit. She needed to speak her peace and get the truth out, so she did. She explained how Rasheed presented the idea to her while they had been drinking one night. The conversation turned to Senaj and Rasheed expressed his distaste about Reign to her. She admitted that what she heard from Rasheed left a bad taste in her mouth and everything in her body wanted to ruin what Senaj and Reign had - that was, until she found out that she was pregnant. When she told Rasheed, he disregarded what she had said. Two days later was when Senaj had texted her mistaking her for Reign. Rasheed was the one who convinced her to go along. At that point she was through with Rasheed, but he threatened to put his hands on her. To protect herself, she did what Rasheed told her to do.

"So why are you telling us this?" Senaj asked, beyond pissed at what he was hearing. His best friend was betraying him right in front of his face. He wondered if Polite knew what was going on.

"Because I know it's wrong. I know that you two are happy. I know that I shouldn't have had sex with Senaj and I just want to right my wrongs. Rasheed is jealous of what you guys have. He doesn't like Reign. I fed into that because I wasn't thinking for myself. When I saw that Senaj was going to be my son's doctor, all of these old feelings came back. Yes, I wanted him to be mine again, but it got to be too much when

I made the mistake of telling Rasheed. I wholeheartedly apologize for my actions and can only give both of you my word that I will never bother you guys again," Christina finished. By the end of her explanation, she was dabbing tears from her eyes - not the fake cry like women who know they are wrong, but don't want to actually admit to themselves that they were wrong, but actual heartfelt tears.

Reign sighed. At times she wanted to be as tough and as heartless as a nigga, but moments like this, she felt like a woman. She couldn't understand what it was like to have a nigga thinking for her, but she knew that women went through shit like this. One thing she hated was the fact that men like Rasheed preyed on women like Christina. *Fuck*, she thought to herself.

"Does Rasheed know that you were coming to speak with us?" Senaj asked.

"No," Christina responded, patting her eyes dry.

"Keep it that way," Reign spoke.

Christina saw the sneer on her face and knew that nothing good was going to come from this.

"I just need one thing from you, Senaj," Christina said.

"What's that?" His voice was laced with confusion.

"I know you're not the baby's father, but I would still like it if you took a DNA test only so that I can prove it to Rasheed. I'm paying for everything, so all you have to do is show up."

"If you know he's not the father, why does he - "

"I'll go. Just let me know what time, where, and what day," Senaj spoke cutting Reign off and side-eyeing her.

Reign's mouth slid open in shock just a tad bit beginning to decide to protest. Her mind told her to shut it.

"Are we done here?" Reign asked instead. She didn't have an appetite and was ready to go. Even if she did have one, she wouldn't sit there and share a meal with the woman who tried to sabotage her relationship.

Reign watched as Christina nodded her head. Going inside her pocket, she threw a hundred dollars bill on the table and began to place Zariyah back into her snow suit. Senaj followed by getting Kahlil ready.

Christina sat with her head down, relieved that she had gotten her confession off of her chest. She couldn't help but be concerned as to what Rasheed would do if he found out what she had done. *I just got to deal with it when it comes to that bridge*, she thought. She watched as Reign and Senaj walked out of the restaurant, praying silently to God to place forgiveness in their hearts.

Mimi

Chapter Seven

Thomas, who was known on the streets as Dice due to his lucky streak of winning every game of cee-lo, was making his last rounds of collecting money before calling it a night. The streets were deserted due to the recent snowfall, but that didn't matter to the dope boys or dope fiends. Usually Thomas would have his speakers booming with the latest hip hop album, but he decided to mellow it out with the sounds of *The Miseducation of Lauryn Hill*. Don't get it twisted, he was a savage, but he liked his music smooth at times.

Thomas pulled up in front of 222 Pulaski Street in Bed-Stuy, parking his car to pull out his cell phone. A motorcycle approaching caused him to look up cautiously, but it continued down the street. By the plump ass and tight leather outfit, he knew it was a female. He shook his head at the craziness. It was damn near ten degrees outside and slippery as hell outside and shorty was on a motorcycle. Shaking his head yet again, he diverted his attention back to his phone.

"Aye yo. I'm downstairs. Bring me that pack," Thomas said into his phone.

"I'll be down," the person answered on the other end of the phone.

Thomas got comfortable as he anticipated the wait. His worker – well, this one anyway - had the tendency to take forever, which is why he always saved him last. As much as he hated to wait, his money was always right, so he never complained.

Thomas scrolled through Instagram while he waited, thinking about the food that he had waiting for him at home. He preferred to have a woman waiting, but he was in between them as if he was in between jobs.

A figure moving towards his car caught the corner of his eye and he began to roll down his window.

"My bad for taking so long," his worker stated as he gave him some dap through the window.

"Man, you say that every time I come pick up from your ass. My money always being straight is the only reason why I tolerate it."

"You done for the night?"

"Yeah, man. It's slow tonight. This snow killing my pockets."

"I feel you. The last two hours were hella slow. Hopefully it picks back up at midnight. If not, I'm just gonna call it a night."

The sound of the motorcycle cut their conversation as they both peered to see it fly past them. Thomas noted that it was the same one from before. With an ass like that he wouldn't forget it. He placed his hand through the window to give his worker a farewell dap.

"A'ight I'm gonna get up out of here. Running the street all day got a nigga stomach touching his back, ya feel me?"

"A'ight, I'll holla at you later," the worker responded with a dap.

Thomas made sure that he was away from the car before he completely moved from his car. He turned up Lauryn Hill and mad a beeline for his house.

Thomas pulled into the garage that was attached to his building on Little West Street and took a minute to get out of the car. The beginning and the end of his day was always spent in prayer. He wasn't a religious man, but he had to thank God for allowing him to be put in such a high power. Even if it didn't make sense that was praying to God to push poison.

Grabbing his things from the car, he proceeded to head to the elevator doors. What he didn't know was that death was lurking behind the elevator doors. He pressed the up button with his head down, looking into his phone.

A small but strong hand wrapped around his throat and brought him to attention as he looked into the prettiest brown eyes. His eyes roamed up and down her body and he instantly realized that this was the same girl that was on the motorcycle. She smiled at him, something evil. He was so caught in her beauty that he forgot that he couldn't breathe. The items he had in his hands dropped as he wrapped his hands around her arm trying to loosen her grip. It did absolutely nothing.

"You have been stepping on someone's toes. And they don't like it. I've been told that you've been warned on several instances, but you are still trying to muscle your way onto blocks that don't belong to you," Reign stated, still with a smile on her face.

Thomas thought this bitch was crazy and the only thought was that he needed to have her on his team. "You…crazy…but…I…will…look…past…this…and…put …you…on…my…payroll," he managed to say.

The smile was still on Reign's face, but showed him amusement.

"If you can offer me more than fifty thousand for each hit, then I can drop my hand right now and we could forget about this little mishap. How does that sound?"

Thomas had money, but not that kind of money. He knew he stepped on quite a few people's toes, but he only knew of one person who had the kind of money to hire somebody to murder him. His heart thundered in his chest because he knew that this was his fate. He figured that he would fight to the death. He tried to jab her, but was met with a punch to his gut that knocked the little bit of wind that he had in him out of him.

Reign allowed him to crumple to the floor and stood over him, waiting to realize that she had sunk a six-inch Schrade knife that curved into his gut. His breathing was ragged and Reign enjoyed watching the realization hit him that he had a knife lodged into his stomach.

"I didn't think that you did. Jameson sends his regards," she said menacingly, grabbing the finger slot and sliding the knife upwards, spilling his guts all over the garage floor. After he stopped gurgling, she took the knife out of his body and placed it into a Ziploc bag that she had hidden in her back pocket. She opened the bag Thomas had been carrying and saw money inside. The bag was maybe as big as a large clutch, so she knew wasn't much was in the bag. She placed the Ziploc in the bag with the money and proceeded to draw a heart on his wrist. Satisfied with her work, she bent the corner and got on her bike to go fuck the shit out of Senaj.

***

Senaj was knocked out, mouth open and all, when Reign got back. After she had checked on the kids, she walked inside the master bathroom and turned her shower on. Her cell phone vibrated, a text from Jameson letting her know that he approved of her job and then another notification popped up letting her know she had money deposited into her account – an offshore account that she had set up after the death of her uncle. The smile on her face showed that she was pleased.

Pulling back the shower curtain, she stepped into the steaming hot water that did justice to her achy muscles. Reign quickly washed with Dove body wash and got out. Since she had killed Thomas, she was experiencing tingling in her vagina that she had never experienced before. She needed Senaj in a bad way and it didn't matter if he had to go to work in the morning. She was going to get that dick one way or another. When she was out of the shower, she placed her hair in a ponytail and moisturized her skin with coconut oil. After dropping her towel in the hamper, she walked as naked as the day she was born into their bedroom. Senaj was laying on his back in only silk pajama bottoms and even though he was soft, the print that was on display made her mouth water. Reign moved closer to the bed and slowly climbed into it, making sure that she didn't wake Senaj. The way his mouth hung open, she doubted that he would easily wake up. For a moment, she admired his body and the way his skin laid smoothly across his body structure. She appreciated it. Reign pulled the band of his pants and boxer briefs down low enough to reach her hand in and fished out his soft penis.

Reign positioned herself onto her knees, on the side of him, and kissed his head. She peeked at him to see if he so much as moved, but he didn't. She held his penis in her hand and wrapped her lips on the head and sucked, tightening her lips to make it feel like he was entering her grade-A tight pussy. Moments later, she began to get a reaction and he was growing in her mouth. She effortlessly slid him down her throat and performed fellatio so damn good that it would probably wake a dead man.

"Sss...damn, babe," Senaj moaned while laying his hand on top of her head.

Reign's mouth was too full to respond, so she looked up at him and winked. Reign knew that he was on the verge of cumming when she noticed his toes started to curl. Her jaws tightened around his penis. She wanted to stop so she could satisfy her body, but she was enjoying sucking his dick and the feeling of her pussy dripping from it.

"Mmm...babe, stop right quick. Put your pussy in my face," Senaj moaned.

Without hesitation, she opened her legs and placed them on either side of his torso. Senaj grabbed Reign by her thighs and placed her pussy over his mouth. Senaj wrapped his arms under her thighs and brought his hand around to spread her ass cheeks and lift her lower part of her body at the right angle so his mouth reached her perfectly. His tongue slid up and down her slit, causing Reign to pause and wind her waist on his tongue slowly. Saliva dripped from her mouth to his dick due it just being in her throat.

"Ooh fuck! Yes!" Reign moaned.

Senaj's mouth was wrapped around her clit while his tongue was flicking across her bean. Reign altogether forgot about sucking his dick. She couldn't focus. She rested her palms on Senaj's thighs and arched her back. She threw her head back, enjoying the sensation that Senaj was providing. She was seconds away from causing a waterfall down his face.

"Go ahead and let it go, babe," Senaj coached as he removed his mouth away from her pussy momentarily. He stuck his thick tongue in her pussy while rubbing and applying pressure in circular motions.

Reign felt the sweat forming on her lower back as she came all over his face. Her eyes rolled to the back of her head as she moaned with pleasure. Senaj kept sucking her clit until she was tapping out. Literally, she had to stop. Reign crumpled to the side of Senaj, landing on the bed, causing Senaj to chuckle.

"Oh my God!" Reign spoke as her legs shook.

"Are you done?"

Reign looked Senaj in his eyes and then down at his rock-hard dick. She responded, "You know I'm not done until I get him back down."

Senaj chuckled yet again and balanced himself on his knees. Reign scooted to the middle of the bed and spread her legs to give Senaj a bird's eye view of her clean-shaven pussy. She jumped slightly as he ran her finger across her clit because it was slightly sore. Senaj wore a smile so big. He didn't know how he could be so lucky with a girl like Reign. Senaj kissed her luscious lips and smacked her thigh to signal for Reign to turn over onto her stomach, and she assumed the position. Her breasts were on the bed as her arms were stretched out above her head and her back was arched, tooting her ass high in the air. Senaj couldn't help himself as he spread her ass cheeks and licked from her pussy hole and over her asshole and up her crack.

Senaj held his dick and slid up and down her slit, coating it in wetness. He slid his dick inside of her and grabbed handfuls of ass and moved his pelvis to smash into her pussy. Senaj was digging in her pussy so good, she was grabbing at the pillows trying to run away. Senaj let her ass cheeks go and grabbed her ponytail with one hand and used the other to wrap it around her neck. She couldn't move, but it was so pleasurable. Her moaning increased as Senaj dug deep into her guts, hitting her spot.

"Oh fuck! I'm gonna cum, Senaj!" Reign moaned out.

"Me too, babe," Senaj responded. He repositioned himself onto the balls of his feet and pulled Reign into him.

He felt himself getting ready to cum. Not wanting to risk Reign getting pregnant again so soon, Senaj pulled out and stroked himself until his kids landed on Reign's ass and back. Her juices leaked down her legs as she heard the sink water turn on in the bathroom. Reign laid on her back as she watched Senaj come back inside of the room with a warm wash rag. Sitting on the bed, Senaj pushed Reign's legs open and used the rag to wash their sex away. Senaj leaned over and placed a kiss on Reign's forehead. Within seconds, he placed the rag back in the bathroom and came back. He was lying on his back when Reign, with a smile on her face, rolled over to cuddle up with him.

Senaj rubbed his hand across her curves as his mind swirled with questions. He looked down into her face and asked, "Where did you go tonight?"

Chapter Eight

"Do you think this is the right thing to do?" Jackie asked Akuchi.

They were sitting in the county clerk's office in Brooklyn. With them was Jamori and his girlfriend, whom they had the pleasure of meeting just hours ago. Her name was Tina and she seemed cool. She was a Southern Belle, hailing from New Iberia, Louisiana, and was studying biomedical engineering at NYU. Jamori was the toughest dude that Jackie knew, but when he was around Tina, he was a different person. He constantly wore a smile on his face.

"This is as right as it's gonna get. Don't tell me you changing your mind?" Akuchi asked.

"No. Of course not. I'm just a little nervous."

Akuchi smiled at Jackie and said, "Jamori got him someone, Reign and Senaj got each other and the kids...what are we going to have? If you trust me, we are going to be straight, but I no longer want you to be my girlfriend. I want you to carry my name."

"Akuchi and Jacqueline." A woman's voice cut through their conversation.

Akuchi looked at Jackie to let her know that everything would be okay. He grabbed her hand as they all stood up and followed the officiant into the room. Akuchi noticed how nervous Jackie was just by her sweaty palms and smiled. He squeezed her hand to reassure her that everything was going to be okay. Jackie looked at Akuchi and placed a smile on her face, and swallowing what little spit that she had, she shook her nervousness off. Jamori and Tina stood off to the side and watched with smiles on their faces. The officiant told Akuchi and Jackie to face one another and hold each other hands.

"Repeat after me," the officiant said. She had a bright smile on her face and you could tell that she enjoyed her job. The smile on her face was so big that she was borderline looking crazy.

Jackie went first. Nervously she looked up at Akuchi and got lost in his eyes. All nervousness and doubt flew from her mind as she began, "I, Jacqueline, take you, Akuchi, to be my husband, to have and to hold from this day forward, for better or for worse, for richer, for poorer, in sickness and in health, to love and to cherish; from this day forward until death do us part."

Tears ran down her face unexpectedly and she quickly brushed her hand across her face. She hated to cry and she was hating the fact that the tears were freely falling. It was now Akuchi's turn. He was just as nervous as Jackie, but he didn't show it. The tears in his eyes welled up in the corners, threatening to fall. He got down on one knee and recited his vows. Unexpectedly, Akuchi pulled out a black velvet box that obviously held a ring inside. When he opened the box, both Jackie's and Tina's mouths dropped in surprise. In the box was a 14K rose gold 1.2 carat princess sapphire diamond wedding band and engagement ring.

"What are you doing? How did you get a ring if we weren't going to do them?" Jackie asked.

"I know that this was a spur of the moment kind of thing, but I've been knowing for quite some time now that I've wanted to marry you. So, I got these a while ago and couldn't figure out when was going to be the perfect time. Rings don't show how much I love you, but I knew that I couldn't make you my wife without making this complete and perfect, so I bought these rings. Besides that, I don't need you around your friends bashing me for not getting you a ring."

"Oh, shut up. That could never happen. But I have something for you, so stand up." Jackie stated. From her purse, she retrieved a black velvet box containing a ring. She opened it and revealed a 14K rose gold and ebony wood wedding band with a diamond in the center.

"How crazy is it that we both picked out rings that almost match?" Akuchi questioned with laughter. The tears by now had dropped from his eyes.

"I would love it for you to enjoy this moment for as long as you can, but in this current moment there are others waiting to experience what you are," the officiant stated, interrupting their brief conversation.

Placing their rings on each other fingers they said their "I do's", signed the marriage certificate, and were pronounced Mr. and Mrs. Ademyemi.

"I love you so much that my heart aches at the thought of ever losing you," Akuchi mentioned with his lips on hers.

Jackie pulled away from Akuchi and asked, "Oh shit. Reign and Senaj, when are we going to tell them?"

"I have a surprise for everyone in the next few days. We'll tell them then."

Jackie didn't feel right keeping this news from Reign, but she was going to follow his lead. Leaving the court house, the sun was shining down on them, even if it was cold. Nothing could ruin this happy moment for them.

***

Reign was sitting at the kitchen table with her arms folded as she watched Senaj move around the kitchen, getting ready for work. The kids, thankfully, were still sleeping and Jackie, Akuchi, and Jamori were gone. Senaj had his tie thrown across his shoulder, pouring milk inside his coffee.

"I don't understand why you're sitting there with your arms folded and your face screwed up. You shouldn't be mad," Senaj said as he sipped from his mug.

"I'm mad because you're making a big deal out of it."

"And you think that I shouldn't? We had this conversation and you told me that you wouldn't do this no more," Senaj stated.

The previous night he fell asleep before Reign and he didn't know that she had received the phone call letting her know that she had to complete her mission, or she would be out of the fifty thousand that was placed on Thomas's head. She told Jameson to give her an hour and she was on it. The kids were up at the time and she had to make sure they were asleep before she went anywhere. Zariyah had woken up crying and Senaj woke up from his sleep to go check on her. That was when he realized that Reign was missing. While they were talking, he was calm about it, but he was boiling on the inside. He knew at any moment, she could possibly get hurt, be sent to jail, or even die. He wanted his kids to have both of their parents and he felt she was being selfish.

"This has been my life, Senaj. You've known about this for how long now? It's not just easy to up and stop if I've been doing this for years. Even before you."

"Reign, you could try to reason and make it try to make sense, but you and I both know that it doesn't. It's senseless and you know that."

Reign sighed. She knew that she couldn't and wouldn't get through to Senaj. What she was doing was wrong and she knew it, but at the same time, she had to do what she had to do for her family. Senaj was a doctor, but even if she didn't say it out loud, she knew that he wasn't making enough money yet, not like she was. For one hit she was making fifty thousand. Her account was sitting lovely at close to a million dollars. If she wanted to, she could have told him that he didn't have to work. Senaj was a man's man and felt like he needed to be in charge with taking care of his family. Talking about this was not how she wanted to spend her morning.

Senaj looked at Reign and his heart thundered in his chest. His heart reacted that way every time he looked at her because he loved her. Probably even more than he loved himself. Before he allowed this situation to get more heated than what it was, he decided to put space between them. Placing his mug in the sink, Senaj placed a kiss on Reign's forehead and walked out, leaving Reign with her thoughts.

Mimi

Chapter Nine

Throughout the day for Senaj, it was hard for him to focus. He was going through his day in a haze and couldn't remember much about what was going on with his patients. Lunchtime rolled around and he figured that he would stay in his office and catch up on his paperwork. His appetite was non-existent at this point, but the fresh cup of coffee that he had purchased was doing him justice. Senaj was so immersed in his work that he didn't realize that someone was standing in his open doorway until they caught his attention by knocking on the door. Senaj slightly jumped but when he realized who it was, he smiled.

"Yo, it's been a minute since I've seen your black ass," Senaj expressed as he got up to give Polite dap.

"Fool, you became a doctor and got too big for the little people." Polite took a seat.

"Nah. Me becoming a doctor had nothing to do with it. It's just a small piece. You have yet to come see your godchildren since your goddaughter has been home from the hospital."

You are right, so I can't give you grief." Polite laughed, but continued, "We've both been busy so we can let each other slide. How's the family?"

"The family is good, man. I'd never thought that I would be the father to not one, but two kids. Even if Kahlil ain't mine biologically, I'm still glad to have him as mine."

"I'm proud of you, man. I don't know if I've told you but I am. We've all grown up and became men and handling what we got to handle. We didn't become statistics and I love that about us, man. You became a doctor, I got my clothing stores up and running, and Rasheed busting his ass at sanitation. Well, last I heard from him he was. Have you spoken to him?"

Senaj's eyes darkened at just the sound of his name being spoken. He never thought that he would hate to hear his once best friend's name being spoken. He remembered the day Christina told him how foul Rasheed had become and got angry all over again.

"I haven't spoken to that fuck boy in a while," Senaj spat.

"Whoa! You know he is your best friend, right?"

"Ain't no best friend of mine gonna try to sabotage my relationship. You my best friend, are you trying to sabotage my relationship?"

"Nah, because I don't get down like that. Bring that back for me though. How is he trying to sabotage what you got going with Reign? Y'all got kids together. I just can't see him doing no shit like that."

"I thought the same thing until I found out that he was," Senaj replied snidely. He began to tell Polite what he knew from Christina.

Polite couldn't believe what he was hearing. Granted, Polite had an issue with Senaj being with Reign when he found out what she did for a living, but he would never go through the lengths that Rasheed was to see them in part. In fact, he wouldn't do anything to break them up. He knew that his best friend was in love with Reign and there was absolutely nothing that he could do about it, so he accepted it. By the time Senaj finished telling him everything, he was flabbergasted.

"Bro, I'm speechless. I can't believe this," Polite spoke. He honestly didn't know what to say.

"And that is exactly why I called him a fuck boy. If I was to see dude, he is liable to catch a case of these hands."

"Maybe if I talk to him - "

Senaj interrupted, "Polite, it's too late to talk to him. There is no coming back from that. Don't get me wrong, I get that y'all had y'all opinions on my relationship with Reign. But as people, there is nothing that not only you and him or anyone could do about our relationship. Not even my mother could do anything, and please believe, she tried. For him to go out his way and drag Christina into it was beyond fucked up, and I could never forgive him for that. I don't want you being thrown in the middle of this, so no, don't talk to him about nothing. The friendship is dead; ain't no need to revive it."

"When are you going to take the DNA test?" Polite asked, switching the subject from off of Rasheed.

"Christina texted me the other day and let me know the test was scheduled Tuesday, next week."

"You want me to go? You know you may run into him and I would hate for either one of y'all to go to jail. Y'all both know that I am the level headed one out of the bunch."

"You can show up, but most likely Reign is going to be there because she doesn't fuck with Christina."

"A'ight bet. Bring the kids too. I'd like to see them."

"You got it."

Polite stood up from his seat and reached his hand out to Senaj to dap him up before making his exit. Senaj got back to work once Polite was out of the room. His mind wasn't at ease after he had to speak about Rasheed's disloyalty. He needed to speak with Reign because what Senaj didn't tell Polite was that he hasn't even mentioned the text to Reign. She would lose her mind if she found out. He picked his phone up, scrolled to her name, and hit the call button.

"Hello," she answered sleepily.

"Hey babe. Were you napping?" he asked.

"Kind of. The kids were napping and I was supposed to be catching up on my shows. Instead, they were watching me."

"Well then, I won't keep you long. I just wanted to let you know that Christina texted me to let me know the date for the DNA test. It's next Tuesday."

There was a brief silence as Senaj waited for Reign to say something. He would have taken her yelling and cursing, anything besides the uncomfortable silence that was going on.

Finally, she spoke. "Okay. Do you want me to come with you?"

"Of course. Why would you ask that?"

Reign's voice was small when she said, "Because of what is going on between us right now."

"It's two different things. I would expect you to come. In fact, I doubt that you even wanted to ask me if I wanted you to come. Even if I told you no, you still would have come. But I'll let you slide with that. We'll talk when I get him. I gotta run," Senaj spoke. While he missed Reign, he was still upset with her and he didn't want to give her the satisfaction of thinking that she had won. He was wrong for hanging up on her, but he figured that that should have been the least of her worries. She'd be fine.

Two days later...

Akuchi woke up bright and early on Saturday. The sun hadn't even touched the horizon yet and he was up. Carefully he slid out of the bed, away from Jackie, careful not to wake her. He went into the hallway bathroom and brushed his teeth and washed his face. He had the perfect surprise for everyone and he needed to be up this early to get everything together. Once he was done in the bathroom, Akuchi quietly went down the stairs to the kitchen. The house was silent as he went into the fridge and cabinets, getting everything he needed to create some of his childhood favorite meals.

Akuchi was making Saso, which was chicken and rice; Mikate; deep fried dough balls; porgies in peanut sauce; spicy broiled prawns, and dessert was baked bananas coated in bread crumbs and would be served with sour cream and brown sugar. It had been ages since he had authentic African cuisine, since he had been locked up for most of his life. Since he had been out of prison, he had been eating and cooking American-ized food, and while he didn't think it was nasty, he wanted what he grew up on.

African food took time to make, which is why he had got-ten up so early to start. Akuchi wanted to not only make these dishes the right way, but also make them delicious. After all, this would be his wife's first time experiencing a part of his culture. He wanted things to be perfect.

Around nine o' clock the house started to wake up and naturally everyone sauntered into the kitchen. Everyone was surprised to see Akuchi in the kitchen. When Senaj saw what Akuchi was cooking, excitement coursed through his body.

"Nah, bro. You serious? Tu cuisine vraiment c'est?" Senaj excitedly asked. He was so excited for this meal that he re-verted back to their native French tongue. He simply asked if he was really cooking this delicious meal. Jackie, Jamori, and Reign stood there watching the brothers share their excite-ment.

"That last time I had any food with the taste of home was before I went to prison. It's been too long. It's Saturday and everyone is finally home together. So I thought, why not?" Akuchi stated as he went to lift the lid from the pot to check on the porgies.

"Everything smells so damn good," Jamori stated, taking a bowl from the cabinet to make himself a bowl of cereal.

"I can agree with that. Good morning, baby," Jackie said. She walked behind Akuchi and wrapped her arms around his waist and placed kisses on his back. A smile formed on his face as he lovingly caressed her hands.

"Ewww. Get a room," Reign exaggerated while making Zariyah a bottle.

Senaj was busying himself getting together oatmeal together to feed Kahlil. Without a response from Jackie or Akuchi, Reign went to go join Jamori in the living room.

"Where you been hiding out at, cousin? I barely see you," Reign asked, taking a seat on the couch. She adjusted Zariyah on her lap to feed her.

"I've just been chilling. Finding myself, trying to adjust to New York and see where I fit in."

"You need anything?"

"Nah. I ran into some dudes and they put me on, if you know what I mean. I'm straight for right now."

Reign wanted to know who it was that he had met. She needed to make sure that her cousin was good, but she knew deep in her heart that he could take care of himself. She decided to change the subject. If she needed to know anything further, she would just simply ask.

"Oh, I know what it was that I was supposed to ask you. Who is this girl that you have been spending time with?" she asked, nudging him.

He couldn't help the smile that stretched across his face. He was smiling so hard that the milk and cereal that he was chomping on spilled from the corners of his mouth. After he swallowed the cereal, he said, "Her name is Tina."

"From the looks of it, she got you wrapped around her pinky finger. Any female that can make a nigga smile the way you just did got his heart," Reign stated. She knew the look all too well. Both she and Senaj, despite their issues, smiled at each other the same way.

"She's pretty decent," Jamori answered simply. Even though she was going to come over later, he still didn't want to talk about her.

"Ugh! What do you mean that she is pretty decent? What is up with y'all dudes? If you digging her, just say so instead of just saying something so simple as 'she's decent'. She's pretty fucking dope if y'all niggas spending y'all time with her. So pretty decent ain't gonna fly by me."

Jamori knew that Reign was right, so he admitted it, "You right. And you know what? Tina is pretty fucking dope. It's hard for me to talk about anyone that I'm dealing with because the last person I fell in love with showed me she was disloyal as fuck. I opened up about her with Nana and Jackie, they met her, had girls' day with her, the whole nine. You know what she did? She went behind my back and fucked my homeboy. The only nigga that I ever considered family. Tina is going to be here today and she's gonna meet everyone. I don't have any friends in New York so I know I won't get hurt again like that. When she's with me, she doesn't even look at another nigga, so I know I can trust her - for now."

Reign was shocked that he had opened up about his ex. She could only imagine how devasted Jamori was behind that. She was glad that he was able to find love again with Tina. Reign had been through something similar with her ex, Josiah.

"I can definitely understand where you are coming from. Before Senaj, a nigga named Josiah was why I didn't want to fall in love again. I gave him every vulnerable piece of me and I ended up catching him in our bed with a tranny. My heart was shattered. How could I not see the signs? For years, I wouldn't let another nigga next to me. I didn't trust them. Eventually, I met Senaj and he changed everything for me. Every time I look at that man, my heart pounds in my chest. He is the only man that I could see myself with. Someday, I would like to marry that man and have all of his babies that he wants me to have. Senaj changed everything for me and I believe that Tina will change everything for you," Reign expressed. A tear welled in the corner of her eye because she knew that if she kept working for Jameson, there could be a possibility that it wouldn't happen.

"That's deep, Reign. Everybody deserves a second chance at love. I had to learn the hard way that not all people are the same. I can't wait for y'all to meet Tina. She's the total opposite of you and Jackie."

Reign placed Zariyah on her shoulder to burp her and side-eyed Jamori for his comment. She asked, "Just what the fuck you mean by that?"

"Exactly how you took it. Y'all are loud and kind of ratchet at times. Tina is reserved, quiet unless she is talking about something that she is passionate about, and she is even quite shy. So please, when you and Jackie meet her, if y'all hang with her, don't turn her into y'all."

Reign's mouth dropped as Jamori walked out of the living room and back into the kitchen. Reign shook her head and finished burping Zariyah before decided to head upstairs to get ready for the day.

Senaj was still downstairs with Kahlil and Zariyah had dozed off back to sleep in her crib. If Reign was going to be able to shower, now would be the time to do so. Sweats and a T-shirt had become Reign's lounging clothes since she'd become a mother, but today, she thought that she'd switch it up. She took out a pair of blue jean distressed pants that hung loosely off of her waist. She grabbed a fitted pink V-neck short sleeved shirt with matching pink socks. Afterward, she headed into the bathroom to take a shower.

"Babe." She heard Senaj calling her name just as she was lathering soap on her wash rag.

"In the shower," she called back.

His footsteps let her know that he was making his way into the bathroom. A breeze crawling over her body caused her to shiver and turn to her left. She saw Senaj standing there holding the shower curtain back.

"Kahlil is downstairs with Jackie I was checking to see how you were doing and if you needed anything."

"Thank you, but I'm okay. Oh, wait, I took my clothes out, but I forgot to grab me some panties and a bra. Can you do that for me please?"

"Ooh, yeah. I'm gonna pick out my favorite ones and then I'm going to come and join you," Senaj spoke with flirtation in his voice.

He left the bathroom and took out a matching burgundy lace bralette and matching boy shorts. Stripping out of his clothes, he went back inside of the bathroom and joined Reign in the shower. Senaj stood under the stream of water as he looked at Reign. He wrapped his arms around her waist and pulled her to him. She instantly put her head on his chest and melted into him.

"We'll get through this. It won't be like this for long," Senaj said with a kiss to her forehead.

A smile displayed on her face. She believed him and she knew it in her heart. All relationships had rough patches. She knew that they would make it through. Senaj and Reign helped wash each other and got ready to get out of the shower. They entered the bedroom in their towels and got ready for the day.

Knock! Knock!

Senaj opened the door as he looked over his shoulder at Reign to make sure that she was properly covered. She was only in her bralette and boy shorts and in the midst of wrapping her towel around her body as he cracked the door open.

"Food is done, bro. Come down with when y'all done getting ready," Akuchi said with a smile over his face.

"Yo, you good? You've been smiling non-stop since this morning?" Senaj asked his brother. He knew his brother to always be a happy person, but today he was borderline psychotic looking.

"Yeah, I'm straight, bro," he answered, still with that goofy smile. With just that response, he turned and went back downstairs. Senaj closed the door and they continued to get dressed without a word being spoken between the two.

Ten minutes later, Senaj and Reign made it downstairs and noticed a quite a bit of chatter coming from the kitchen. Kahlil was in the dining room in his playpen and when he noticed Senaj, he held onto the sides of his playpen and made his way towards Senaj to throw his hands in the air for Senaj. He wanted to get picked up and like a sucker, Senaj picked him up, causing Kahlil to flash his four baby teeth. He was soon going to be one and they needed to plan his first birthday party soon.

Senaj and Reign made it into the kitchen and noticed three extra people inside the kitchen. Tina had made it as well as Senaj's parents. He didn't expect to see them there due to how it went the last time he had seen them.

"Maman et Papa, tu fais ici?" Senaj asked what they were doing there.

"We haven't seen you in a few months and your first question is what are we doing here?" his mother asked, her hands placed on her hips.

"Of course, I'm happy to see you guys. I guess I'm just a little bit shocked that y'all are here." Senaj drew his mother in for a hug.

Surprisingly, Zain not only hugged him back but she also took Kahlil into her arms. He was a bit fussy at first because he didn't know who she was, but soon settled when she rocked him from side to side. Senaj took that time to embrace his father.

"Hello, Mr. And Mrs. Ademyemi," Reign finally spoke.

The room grew quiet, eerily quiet, and then both Zain and Akachi walked over to Reign and embraced her and Zariyah. Senaj looked at Akuchi, who was smiling brightly, and instantly knew that his brother was behind all of this and why he had been in a good mood.

"Please, you can call us Maman and Papa now. We have things to discuss later, but I would love it if we could just enjoy our grandchildren," Akachi stated. He took Zariyah into his arms. Akachi was usually a serious man and all of Senaj's and Akuchi's life, they had never seen him melt like chocolate until he had taken ahold of Zariyah.

"Senaj and Reign, everyone has met Tina except y'all two. So, Reign and Senaj, this is Tina. Tina, this is my cousin Reign and her dude Senaj," Jamori said. He had taken this opportunity to introduce Tina. He figured that Senaj's parents were pre-occupied with the kids and wouldn't mind holding Reign's and Senaj's attention for a moment.

"It's nice to meet you," Tina said almost bashfully.

"It's nice to meet you as well," Senaj stated with a simple smile and handshake.

Reign walked to Tina and grabbed her into a hug. Jamori slightly rolled his eyes, causing a chuckle from Akuchi.

"Don't be so extra, Reign," Jackie laughed.

"Can I be happy for Jamori? Sheesh."

Reign walked over to the fridge and poured herself some orange juice. Zain and Akachi had disappeared into the living room. As Reign leaned against the counter, sipping on her orange juice, her heart was full. It was only her growing up, so she didn't know how it felt to be in a house full of people. An overwhelming feeling came over her as she began to miss her parents. So much had her occupied that she couldn't remember the last time she had thought about them. She felt bad. It wasn't what she intended but her life had become chaotic. Visiting her parents and her Nana was on the top of her list of things to do. Right after the DNA test.

"Reign? You good?" Jackie asked, noticing the look on Reign's face.

"Oh yeah. I'm good. I just got caught up thinking about my mom and dad. I'm fine."

"You sure?"

"Yeah," Reign stated while putting her cup in the sink.

"You want to help me and Tina set the table?"

Reign smiled, trying to hold back her tears. She replied, "Sure. I didn't realize that we were eating so early."

"Akuchi said that he didn't want to keep his parents out too late and he wanted them to be able to get proper rest," Jackie responded.

Reign simply nodded that she understood. They walked together to get Tina and proceeded to fix the table. Senaj, Jamori, and Akuchi brought out the food, due to how heavy the pots were. Senaj's parents had yet to place the kids down, but Senaj nor Reign complained. After all, this was their first time officially meeting the kids.

Once everyone was seated, food began to get served and Akuchi poured liquor for everyone except his parents. The food was delicious and everyone was licking their fingers to make sure that they didn't miss not one drop or flavor. Since Reign had lost her father, this was all she had wanted: to be able to sit with people that she considered her family. She got lost in her thoughts, thinking yet again about her own parents. The clinking of a glass brought her back to reality.

"Excuse me, y'all," Akuchi spoke, getting everyone's attention.

The chatter in the room died down and all eyes were on him. Akuchi grabbed Jackie by the hand and helped her from her seat. His arm wrapped around her shoulders as her arm went around his waist. No one said anything for several seconds, eyes just darting around trying to figure out what was going on.

"I have some good news, which is why I slaved in a hot-ass kitchen all day. I convinced Mom and Dad to come here because there are things that need to be discussed amongst Reign and Senaj. The most important thing though is that both Jackie and I, just shy of a year of being together, decided to get married. In the beginning, I was kind of skeptical of being around y'all. You know with the whole thing with my brother being kidnapped, but I have actually grown to love y'all," Akuchi said with some of his words slurring due to his drinking.

"When is the wedding?" Zain asked. Excitement laced her voice.

Jackie smiled and held her hand up showing off her ring. She said, "We already had it. Two days ago. We both agreed that we didn't want to do something big, so Jamori and Tina were our witnesses and we decided that this dinner would be our reception."

Reign turned to her right and nudged Jamori, saying, "How could you keep this from me?"

"Because they asked me to keep my mouth shut. That's how secrets work, duh," Jamori explained.

Senaj stood up and walked around the table to Akuchi and grabbed him into a hug. He told him congratulations and how happy he was. Pretty soon everyone was hugging and telling the newlyweds congratulations. As much as Senaj wanted to talk to his parents, he told himself that another day would be fine. This was a celebration for his brother, and that was the only thing that mattered at that moment.

Akachi clinked his glass in the same manner as Akuchi had done to grab everyone's attention. He said, "We were going to wait to share our good news, but it seems like today would be the best day to join in on the celebration. Zain and I decided that we are moving back to New York. It doesn't make any sense to have our family here and we are all the way in Florida. We'd rather not have to see you only a few times out of the year. We will be here for a week finalizing paperwork and within a month, we will be back in New York for good."

Senaj and Akuchi jumped up like two school-aged kids in excitement. There were hugs and laughter in the air and Reign thought, *Maybe giving up working for Jameson wouldn't be too bad.* But she had had these thoughts before. She still ended up working with him. Senaj taking the DNA test was the last issue that they had to come across, and she couldn't wait for that day. If she wanted to remain this happy and content, she knew what she had to do to achieve it.

Chapter Ten
Tuesday

Polite showed up as he said he would. Senaj and Reign waited in silence, looking at the pale blue walls as they waited for Senaj's name to be called. Christina was going to be taking her test at her doctor's office and Rasheed had yet to show up. Polite was enjoying playing with Zariyah and laughing at her when her tiny hands grabbed at his fingers.

"Bro. I need to have me one of these before I end up stealing yours," he said with laughter to Senaj.

"Try it and his hands won't be only ones you gonna catch," Reign responded calmly while flipping through a health magazine.

Polite chuckled and said, "Trust me, I know. She's just too damn cute. She knows that shit too already."

"She is her mother's child," Senaj responded.

There was a nurse that came out and called Senaj. Reign placed a kiss on his cheek as he got up to follow the nurse. Reign's heart sank at the thought of Christina's baby being his. Granted, Christina admitted to having sex with Rasheed two days before Senaj, but that could still mean that there would be a 50/50 chance that the baby was Senaj's. Her stomach felt like it was literally about to fall out of her ass. Taking several breaths, she tried to calm her racing mind.

"Everything is going to be fine," Polite offered. He felt bad that they were going through this. Senaj was wrong for not thinking with his right mind, no matter how drunk he was. He couldn't use the fact that he thought it was Reign. As much time as he and Reign had spent together before that moment, he should know and recognize his woman's voice.

Senaj and Polite hadn't talk to each other much in the last few months, but what Polite knew was that Reign wouldn't cheat on him even for the finest nigga in the world. Even if he wasn't sure that everything was going to be okay, he felt like Reign needed to hear it at the moment.

"I'm just a little nervous. I know that it could possibly be a chance that it's Senaj's," Reign stated. Kahlil was sitting in the double stroller gnawing away at some Wise Puff Cheez-doodles.

"Are you prepared if, God forbid, it comes back as his?" Polite asked.

"What woman is ever prepared for something like this? I don't know what's going to happen, but I did think about it. I told him when we find out and it came back his, I was going to pack up me and the kids and leave. But I know I can't do that. It's just something about Senaj that won't allow me to do him that dirty. I just figured that I could be a sensible adult in this situation and I would just accept the baby and be the best stepmom there is," Reign admitted.

"I'm glad that someone is being sensible. This is a difficult situation that everyone is dealing with. I just hope and pray that things work out for the better."

Reign nodded her head in agreement. Thankfully he was there because those words were the right ones that she needed to hear. She walked the floor of the doctor's office impatiently. She bit her nails as her arms were folded across her chest. Senaj had been in the back for all of ten minutes, but it seemed like hours. He smiled at Reign to reassure her that everything was going to be all good, even if he didn't believe so himself.

With Polite's help, they began to get the kids ready to leave. Rasheed never showed up. They departed from Polite and went to go meet with Zain and Akachi at the Shake Shack in Downtown Brooklyn. They hated to have to drive anywhere in the city. Finding parking was always a bitch.

When they arrived at the restaurant, Zain and Akachi were sitting at a table patiently waiting for them. As Reign maneuvered the stroller through the throngs of tables, Kahlil got excited when he saw his grandparents.

"Looks like someone missed us," Zain mentioned as she reached to unbuckle the safety belt. The smile on his face brought a smile to Reign's face.

"I'm pretty sure that y'all missed them too. I could tell by the way y'all's eyes lit up when you saw them," Reign expressed.

Zariyah was up and beginning to be fussy. It was time for a bottle and Akachi was more than happy to feed his grandbaby.

"I'm so glad that you guys are here. It's great being a parent, but it feels damn good to have a break," Senaj said with a chuckle.

Zain sucked her teeth and said, "You think me and your father had five-minute breaks with you and your brother? You are lucky to have us. We've wanted grandkids for so long that we don't even mind you taking that five-minute break mess you talking about."

"Shall we go to the counter so that we could get some food? This old man is hungry," Akachi said, walking towards Reign to hand Zariyah over.

"Come on, Papa," Senaj said.

The two men walked away from the women and went to place their order for burgers and drinks at the counter.

"You know, I was puzzled at first when you back talked your mother. But you know what I realized and what I had to point out to her? I saw myself in you."

Senaj's eyebrows furrowed and he asked, "What do you mean?"

"Well, when I wanted to be with your maman, your grandfather didn't want her to have nothing to do with me. Growing up, your mother was richer than most in our country and I wasn't. I hung with the troublemakers and did some dirt. I met your mother while she was coming home from school and every moment of her free time was spent with me. When I met your grandfather, he knew that I was trouble. It was like he smelled it all over me. He forbid your mother to see me any longer. He made it harder for her to see me.

"But you know what? That didn't stop either of us. Every day, after she'd get out of school, I was there waiting for her. By this time, I had cleaned up my act, only so that her father would accept me. I stopped hanging with the people who, although they were troublemakers, had my back on many things. She came from out of school one day and greeted me with a smile on her face so bright that in my world it was brighter than the sun. She walked towards me with her arms wide open for me to give her a hug. She dropped them instantly and with her arms went her smile as well. The look on her face said she'd seen a ghost, until I realized that she was looking behind me.

"Your grandfather was standing a few feet away from me with a scowl on his face that said he wanted to kill me. That moment changed my life forever. I stood up to your grandfather and told him how much I loved your mother and there was absolutely nothing that he could do to stop me from doing everything in my power to see your mother."

Senaj was in shock. He'd never heard this story. All that he knew was that his parents were childhood sweethearts. Senaj asked, "What happened after you told Papy that?"

"He dragged your mother away from me. She was kicking and screaming. Even though I had just been acting tough with him, all I could do was look at him drag the love of my life away. I failed her and I knew that I wouldn't see her ever again."

"Well obviously you did, so, how did you?" Senaj asked. He wondered if Akuchi knew this story.

"A month after that, I was home by myself. My maman had gone out on a date with a wealthy man. I knew that she would be away all night, so I picked up one of her favorite books. It was *The Dream Keeper* by Langston Hughes. There was a knock on the door. It was your mother. I didn't recognize her. Your grandfather had beaten on her every day for that month. Her face was twice the size it normally was, her eyes were slits, and her body was covered in bruises. I made sure that your maman would never feel that kind of pain ever again.

"I told you all of that to let you know that we see the love that you have for Reign and understand why you back talked your mother. Your mother and I both came to an agreement that we won't come in between you two unless we have to."

Senaj stood in silence. He needed to know what happened. "Well, what happened to Papy? Did Maman go back to see him?"

The burgers were done and placed on a tray in front of them. Akachi looked at Senaj with a serious look on his face and said, "I killed him."

Akachi grabbed the tray and placed a smile on his face, walking back to the table. Senaj's head was spinning at this information. His father had killed his father-in-law and he didn't know how to feel about it. Senaj snapped out of his daze and joined the rest of his family at the table. Possibly, life could get better for them.

Mimi

Chapter Eleven
Five Weeks Later

Senaj was at work when he had received a phone call from Reign. He couldn't answer the phone because he was with a patient. It must have been an emergency with the way there was text after text was coming in. Silencing his phone until he was done with his patient, he got back into focus. A fourteen-year-old girl was in with her mother due to stomach pains. He examined her and decided that a little gas was building up and he let her mother know that some antacid would clear it right on up. If the pain was to persist after two days, she should bring her back. When he was done, he went back to his office to prepare himself to call Reign back when there was a knock on his office door. When he opened it, he was surprised to see Reign on the other side of the door. *How the hell did she make it here so fast?* he wondered.

"Babe, what are you doing here?" Senaj asked. She was breathing heavy like she had just run a marathon to get here. She had a concerned look on her face. Worry shook his body as he waited for her to say something. She threw her arms around his neck and placed a kiss on his lips. Senaj's eyes widened in surprise as he was confused as to what was going on.

"It's not yours! Dear God, that baby isn't yours," Reign finally said.

"What? Are you serious? Wait, where are the kids?"

Reign took a piece of paper from her back pocket and handed it to Senaj. He looked at the phone and read what Reign had just said. Relief took over his body and he damn near wanted to cry. He had dodged a bullet.

"I'm so, so sorry for putting you through this kind of tor-ture. I can't even begin to think what you were going through while dealing with this. I will never do anything to ever make you feel like you can't trust me. I love you with everything in my body, Reign," Senaj said while holding her hands in his. He wrapped one of his hands around the back of her neck and pulled her in for a kiss. They kissed as if they were hungry for each other.

Senaj pushed Reign against the door and locked it. His hand went to the front of her neck and he squeezed softly, causing Reign to moan out in pleasure. His dick was hard as a rock and was begging to be released from his pants. While they kissed, Senaj unbuttoned her pants and pulled them down to her ankles. He turned her around and made her place her hands on his desk as her ass was in the air. He paused for a moment to admire her smooth chocolate skin. Quickly, his pants and boxers fell to his ankles. Spreading Reign's ass cheeks, he guided himself inside of her, pausing to savor that moment. Granted, they had sex often, but her pussy was always tight and gripped his dick just right. Both Reign and Senaj hated quickies, but it would have to do in this heated moment. Senaj dug deep in Reign's insides for several minutes when he felt her leaking juices splashing against him.

"Damn, babe," Senaj moaned.

Senaj could have sworn that she was the wettest that she had ever been. He felt his nut building up. He took his dick out of her and sat on his chair. Reign turned around, her back towards him, and sat on his dick. Senaj lifted her shirt up, pulling her bra in the process, and rubbed his fingers across her nipples. Her walls tightened around his dick with each bounce.

"You getting ready to cum, babe?" Reign moaned.

"Mm hmm," he moaned.

Reign jumped from off of his dick and got on her knees in front of him. Senaj stroked his dick as he watched Reign open her mouth. He loved when she did freaky shit. She was waiting for Senaj's nut with her tongue out, grabbing and rubbing on her titties. Within seconds he was letting his nut go. It was a big one too, landing everywhere except for its intended spot. Reign used her fingers to grab what she could and licked her fingers clean.

"You nasty," Senaj said with a chuckle.

"But you love it when I get nasty. I don't ever hear you complain," she said, getting up from the floor and fixing her clothes.

"I would be a fool if I did."

Senaj watched Reign get dressed. Everything about her he had loved, and he wouldn't change a thing - except for her occupation. This was who he had fallen in love with. Second guessing himself and asking her to stop, he wondered, if the shoe was on the other foot, would she stop fucking with him?

Reign smiled when she noticed that Senaj was looking at her. She walked over to him to say her good byes. Her arms went around his neck and she inhaled his scent. Dolce and Gabbana's The One mixed with the faint scent of sweat.

"I love you and I'll see you when you get home," Reign said while biting her bottom lip. She could go another round, but she knew he had to work. Waiting until he got home was a sacrifice that she would gladly accept.

"I love you too. Kiss the kids for me."

After Reign left the room, he got himself together to get ready for the rest of his day. He was only halfway through his day and that quickie was about to put him in a pussy coma. Good – no, immaculate pussy - would do that to you. He shook that sleepiness off with a cup of coffee and got back to work.

***

Six o' clock had finally come for Senaj and it was time for him to call it a day. His last patient was a girl he used to mentor. He recognized her as soon as he saw her. It was Briana, and the last time he had seen her was when she had called him to save her from her mother's boyfriend. He had been molesting her. She stood in front of him that day with her mother, who was telling him that for the past few days she had been throwing up. Her mother was convinced that she was pregnant. He wasn't obligated to give her a pregnancy test, but he did so anyway. Her mother was right and right there in the patient room, her mother broke down crying. She wasn't even sixteen yet and she was carrying a baby. When they left, Senaj's heart was heavy. He felt like he had let her down and possibly any other children at the youth center. He made a vow to himself that he would make it down to the youth center and get back into the habit of being a mentor to the kids there.

Senaj was making his way to his car when he noticed someone was leaning against his car. When he got closer, he noticed that it was Rasheed. He approached Rasheed and stood in front of him waiting for him to speak. His messenger bag hung from his shoulder and his jacket was in his hand. The weather had finally broke and it was slightly warm with a bit of a breeze.

Finally, Rasheed spoke. "You just gonna stand there or are you going to greet a friend that you haven't seen in months?"

"Friend? Are you seriously calling yourself that these days?" Senaj said with a chuckle.

"Whoa, buddy. No need for that. I know we haven't seen or spoken to each other in the last few months, but that don't mean that I don't consider you to be my friend."

"What do you want, Rasheed?"

"For starters, I figured that I'd come check you and see how my friend was doing, to see if you wanted to hit up Smalls like old times to get a few drinks. You know, catch up."

Senaj couldn't help himself from laughing. He couldn't believe that Rasheed was being serious. Senaj walked to the driver side door, opened it, and placed his things inside of the car, all the while still laughing and causing Rasheed confusion.

"Aye, listen here. We ain't got nothing to catch up with. I thought we were friends, but your season is up, my nigga. You know why and you know exactly what you've done to cause this. So, I suggest you get up off my car and go on 'bout your way."

Rasheed pushed himself from off of Senaj's car and stood with his legs slightly spread apart and his hands down by his sides. He said, "Bruh, if you got something to get off your chest, by all means, let it go instead of being a little bitch about it."

"A little bitch? Never that and you know it. This degree and suit and tie ain't changed a motherfucking thing. These hands still work just like when we were younger. And as far as saying what's on my chest, I'd rather not. You know what you did or else you wouldn't be here now. You a lame-ass nigga," Senaj spat.

The tension between Rasheed and Senaj was thick. They stared each other down for several moments. Until Senaj grew tired of this game. He had a family to get home to.

"So that's it? You gonna let Christina get what she wants and put a wedge between our friendship?" Rasheed asked. His voice cracked slightly.

Senaj slammed his car door and walked up on Rasheed, tired of him acting like he had no parts in this whole situation.

"Do not put this on Christina. You used her to manipulate her into trying to break me and Reign up! The only thing that she did was follow your fucking order! I've never known a nigga to be jealous of his friend because he was in a relationship. What the fuck is up with you? Instead of you being happy for a nigga, you out here acting like a whole female!" Senaj yelled.

He'd hit the nail on the head causing something to awaken in Rasheed. Without warning, Rasheed drew his fist back and socked Senaj square in the mouth. Senaj was caught off guard, but it didn't stop him from rocking Rasheed with the worst two piece he'd ever felt. Senaj's blows landed perfectly in the face and throat. Rasheed's head snapped back and before he could fully recover, Senaj delivered several jabs to his abdominal area, knocking the wind out of Rasheed.

Rasheed fell to the ground, struggling to breathe. Senaj stood over Rasheed with his shirt twisted around his hand. Senaj was ready to demolish his face but when he saw Rasheed struggling to breathe, he stopped. Worrying that Rasheed was about to die, he climbed over him and helped him from off of the ground. Senaj then realized that it was the body shots causing Rasheed to act like he was dying.

"Let me tell you something, and you better listen and take heed on this. Stay the fuck away from me and my family if you know what's best for you," Senaj said as he gawked at Rasheed. He had had a genuine love for this dude and he fucked it up.

Senaj turned his gaze from Rasheed and walked to his car. He got in and drove away from someone who he had called a brother his whole life. If he wasn't trying to break up Senaj and Reign, Senaj could have forgiven him easily, but what he'd done was unforgivable. He had to let that toxic friendship go, no matter how much he love his friend.

Senaj didn't realize how much this had taken a toll on him mentally until he felt the wetness from his tears on his cheeks. He would always have love for Rasheed, but he could no longer be his friend, and that was what hurt Senaj the most. On his way home, he wondered if Rasheed had felt any kind of remorse to what he had done. Senaj would never know.

Senaj was supposed to have been home an hour prior, but due to his clouded mind, he went driving around to clear his mind. When he made it home, the house was quiet except for the living room surround sound system blasting a horror movie. He was able to slip inside of the house without being detected and make it upstairs to shower. Once done, he made his way downstairs and went to the kitchen to check for food. Instead, he saw Reign standing with the fridge open, her back to him. He snuck up behind her and wrapped his arms around her face.

"Ahh! Senaj! Why would you scare me like that? Wait, when did you get in?" she asked when she recognized his scent.

"About a half hour ago. I just got done showering," Senaj spoke while placing a kiss on Reign's neck.

She turned around with a smile on her face, but it left as soon as she saw his lips was swollen. "What the fuck wrong with your lip?" She yelled. The TV in the living room was paused and the rest of the gang came inside of the kitchen, including Tina.

"Reign, it's nothing." Senaj knew exactly what would happen if Reign found out Rasheed was behind his lip. He knew blood shed would soon follow.

Akuchi walked up to Senaj and looked his brother in his eyes before he grabbed a hold of his chin and examined his lip.

"What do you mean that it's nothing? I just saw you earlier and it didn't look like that."

Before Senaj could say anything, he saw his brother mouth the words "lie". "After you left, a patient came in with her mother. You remember the girl Briana? The one whose mother boyfriend was molesting her?"

"Yes, I remember," Reign stated. Although it was vaguely, she still admitted to it.

"Her mother suspected that she was pregnant. The test came back positive. Her mom pitched a bitch and as I was helping her up from the floor, she elbowed me," Senaj lied. He hated to not only lie to Reign, but to use Briana's situation and only tell part of the truth. He knew what he needed to do in order to protect Rasheed, even if he felt like he didn't need it. He was mad, not heartless.

Reign stood next to Akuchi, examining Senaj's lip. She sighed and went into the freezer to grab some ice. She made a makeshift ice pack and handed it to him. She said, "Here. This is gonna help the swelling. I can't have you sucking on this pussy with a swollen lip."

Tina and Jackie erupted in laughter as Jamori and Akuchi cursed her out.

"Trust me, a busted lip won't stop me from doing that," Senaj said as Tina, Jackie and Reign left from out of the kitchen to find out what really happened.

"So, you gonna tell us what really happened?" Jamori asked with his head cocked to the side.

"I got into a fight with Rasheed," Senaj began as he continued to tell them what happened.

They shook their heads. Akuchi couldn't believe that Rasheed was going through such lengths to make sure that he made himself look innocent. Akuchi never took Rasheed to be the bitch made type, but no matter how long you think you've known someone, eventually you would see their true colors.

Akuchi vowed to himself that even if it was his last breath, he would make sure that Rasheed would pay for what he'd done to his little brother. By all means, Rasheed would pay.

Mimi

Chapter Twelve

The sun was shining bright and the weather was warm. Spring had showed up and showed out by the time April 14th had come around. Zain and Akachi were settled into their new home in Queens and they had kept Zariyah and Kahlil for the weekend. Reign had something special planned for Senaj and she needed them to be kid free. Senaj had been antsy and wanted to know what Reign was up to. She wouldn't tell him. Senaj and Reign were driving and the only thing that he knew so far was that they were on their way to Glen Cove. He couldn't even begin to think what was in Glen Cove that they needed to be there.

About an hour later, they arrived on Seamon Road. Reign stopped in front of a grey and white family house that was surrounded by a white fence. The grass was super green and Senaj was impressed. He's never seen grass so green. He was still looking at the green grass and didn't realize that Reign had unlocked the door with a key. Inside, the walls were light grey with white trim. Deep brown mahogany wooden floors and high ceilings. There was a fireplace in the living room trimmed with marble tile.

"Whose house we in, and why they ain't got no damn furniture?" Senaj asked. Something wasn't right when he realized they had been there for two whole minutes and nobody came to greet them.

Reign didn't answer Senaj. Instead, she made her way up the stairs, causing Senaj to panic.

"Reign, what the hell are you doing?" Senaj asked in a whisper.

Reign stopped midway up the stairs and said, "I just want to see the bedrooms."

With that, she began to walk up the rest of the stairs. Senaj went back and forth with himself if he should follow Reign up. He followed.

By the time he got to the top of the landing, Reign was nowhere in sight. Senaj began to open room doors, whispering Reign's name, all the while impressed with the size of the bedrooms. He stumbled across a bathroom and couldn't bring himself to immediately close the door. The shower was the length of a full wall with glass doors - not the ones that were foggy, but the ones that you could see through perfectly. The tub sat in the middle of the floor with jets lining the sides. The floor was marble tiled and there were his and hers sinks. Senaj remembered that he was looking for Reign and continued his search. Leaving from the bathroom, he closed the door and made his way to the last room that he hadn't checked. His mouth dropped when he saw Reign standing in the middle of the room. There were flower petals on the floor in the shape of a heart and she was standing in the middle of the heart.

"Reign what are you doing?" Senaj asked.

"Can you come join me in this heart please?" she asked. Her voice was a tad shaky so he knew that she was nervous.

"Of course, babe."

Reign watched as Reign made his way towards her with a smile plastered on her face. She said, "I know you may think that I'm crazy because of how I just walked into this big-ass house like I own it. Truth is, WE own it. I've been bidding back and forth with someone who wanted this house, but I knew I had to have this house for my family. Do you remember how I told you that my dad had left me seven million, but I didn't know where it was?"

"Yes."

"I was cleaning out some of my old things. Things from when I was seventeen. There was a notebook that my father had owned. There was a key taped to the page and an address was written above the key. For a while, I didn't pay it any attention. That was, until I started to think about it more. It kept gnawing at me until one day, I took my ass to the address. It was a building full of storage units. I looked for the unit number that was printed on the key. When I opened the unit, there were trunks on top of trunks full to the top of my parents' things. Things that I never knew existed.

"I didn't know what I was looking for, so I ended up calling it a night. Days passed before I went back. I went the night before you ended up at Christina's. I couldn't sleep. My mind was wondering about many different things. I went back down to the storage unit and I saw a trunk there that had my name on it. I was confused at first because I was pretty sure that I had everything that I had when I left the house."

Reign had been talking fast due to excitement. Senaj was used to it because she did that often. Senaj grabbed her hands into his and didn't want her to explain any further.

"You don't have to explain no more. I get where this is going. All I can say is that I cannot thank you enough for this beautiful house."

Reign kissed his lips and said, "Please let me finish. So, I open the trunk and there is a bunch of little Beanie Babies that I've never seen before. As I picked them up, I realized that there was this black cloth that was covering the something in the truck filled up just above half way. I flipped the cloth back and there was money. As soon as I saw that, I'd remembered seeing two more trunks the same way. Those had cash inside of them as well."

Senaj couldn't believe his ears. You only hear about shit like this happens in movies and books.

Reign continued, "I know we were supposed to do this together but I just felt like since I had the money, why not get it done? I hope that I didn't overstep my boundaries."

A smile spread across Senaj's face. He knew what she meant and who was he to stop her from making sure that her family was good? In response, he said, "You don't have to worry about overstepping your boundaries. If the shoe was on the other foot, I'm pretty sure you wouldn't have a problem with me doing this. Now just one question: when can move in?"

"As soon as possible. This is just the beginning. From the first moment that I've met you Senaj, you have been the most caring, loving, understanding man that I have ever met. I know you don't like what I do, but yet you still don't judge me for it. All you have done was love me for me. I can't thank you enough and, in a way, you have saved me from myself and you don't even know that you've done that. I thank God every morning, noon and night for sending you to me. I don't ever want to see me without you," Reign said. She was full blown crying, trying to keep her composure. Reign went into her pocket and pulled out a ring. She got down on one knee and looked up at Senaj, tears cascading down her face.

"What are you doing?" Senaj asked. He knew what she was doing, but it was the only thing that he could say.

"This ring was my father's. He wore this the day he married my mother. I found it in one of the trunks. I thought it was buried with him. I guess what I'm doing is asking you, Senaj Ademyemi, will you marry me?"

Without hesitation, Senaj answered simply with a yes. This was crazy to him. This was new to him. Men were supposed to be the ones who asked the woman to marry them and was going to do just that once he found the perfect ring. Reign placed the ring on his finger and stood up, sinking her body into his. Senaj hadn't realized it but he shed a few tears too.

Reign placed kisses on his face and hugged him so tightly she never wanted to let go.

"Now how about we look at our new house the right way?" Reign proposed.

"We could do that. I thought you had lost your damn mind walking through somebody else house."

Reign laughed and said, "Your ass was walking around whispering like somebody was going to hear you."

"Shit, I didn't know."

"How about we move in this weekend? We can start after you get out of work Friday? I don't have anything to do this week, I could get Jackie to help me to pack."

"Sounds like a plan to me."

The next day, Reign and Jackie had continued the packing that Reign had started. Reign told her, Jamori, and Akuchi that they were moved in officially, and that they could come over for their first dinner in their new home. Jackie was in complete shock when Reign told her that she proposed to Senaj. After all, it was the man's job to do that. Of course, she thought her cousin was crazy for doing so, but Reign played by her own rules. Reign had just gotten all of her pictures from the walls in the house packed when there was a knock on the door.

"You want to get that or do you want me to get it?" Jackie asked, taking a sip of wine from her glass.

"You can get it. My back hurts from lugging that last box from upstairs."

Jackie got up and laughed her way to the door. She said, "Bitch, that's cause you getting old. Before you know it - "

Jackie's friendly banter halted, causing Reign to jump up to make sure that everything was okay. Jackie was fine, but when she turned to look at Reign, Reign already knew what was going on. The police were at the door.

"Are you Reign Mills?" the first officer asked.

The name on his badge reads Williams. Reign looked at the other one's badge and his read Wick. She couldn't deny who she was. If they came knocking and looking for her specifically, then she knew that they'd done their homework. Her mind went to Senaj and she thought, *Is he okay?*

"Yes, I am. Is it my fiancé? Is he okay?" she finally spoke.

Wick responded, "As far as we know, your fiancé is okay. We are here because we would like to speak with you about Pearl. We understand that you two were friends?"

"Yes, we were. Why would you need to speak with me though? When she passed, I gave the officer that was working her case my statement," Reign said, trying her hardest not to sound nervous.

"There has been some new evidence that has come up in the case and we only want to ask you a few questions. You can come willingly, or we could cuff you and take you the hard way," Williams said while reaching for his cuffs.

"No need to. Let me get some shoes on. Jackie, call Senaj and my lawyer," Reign stated.

She didn't need to move from the door. Her shoes had been right there by the door. She grabbed her jacket and followed them out of the door. A few of the neighbors were outside watching what was going. Reign waited for Wick to open the back door of the squad car in order to climb in. She looked back at her house and saw Jackie on the phone with Jamori and Akuchi by her side. Thank God the kids were with their grandparents.

Chapter Thirteen

Reign was at the precinct, in a cold interrogation room, with the officers who showed up to her house, for several hours. She was pretty sure that it was dark outside now and Reign was trying to figure out what was taking her lawyer so long to get to her. The officers did everything to get her to crack but she knew better. They played good cop/bad cop, then they both played good cop. They even went as far as offering her something to eat. Reign sat there with a smug look on their faces.

"You do know that you aren't under arrest, so you can answer our questions. You are making this process longer than what it needs to be," Wick stated as he stood in a corner with his arms folded.

"I know what I can do, but I won't, because I would feel much more comfortable with my lawyer," Reign responded with her hands folded on top of the table.

"So why don't you tell us what we want to know? We just want to figure out how your relationship was with Pearl, so that we can figure out why she felt like you killed your uncle."

"Because my lawyer isn't here yet."

There was a knock on the door and another officer appeared at the window. Williams opened the door and walked out. He was back in the room in less than five minutes. His face said that he was upset to the max.

"Your lawyer is here and he is causing a scene. We have to let you go. This is far from over, and you will answer out questions one way or another."

"You guys are making it seem like I did something wrong. All you have is words from an old friend, who just so happens to be six feet under. She was pregnant at the time and could have been going through anything emotionally at that point.

119

In this day and age, police are killing black people at such a high rate that I just don't trust being in a room without my lawyer present. I'm not saying that this was the case, because obviously I'm walking away without any harm done to me, but what if I had kept up with being quiet? Would you two have gotten tired of my quietness that y'all would have resulted in beating me? Or possibly accidentally killing me and saying that it was suicide? I don't want to chance it." Reign got up from the table to leave. At the door, she looked back at the officers and smiled at them. They had nothing on her and she knew it.

She followed the third officer down the hall and towards her lawyer. She saw Senaj, Jamori, and Akuchi sitting off to the corner with worried expressions on their faces. She stepped up to her lawyer at the desk and waited until he was done talking to the officer who was stuck doing desk work.

"I will be speaking with your captain soon," Mr. Weinstein spoke in a no-nonsense tone. He turned to Reign and moved her off to the side.

"Babe, you okay?" Senaj asked, standing up.

"Yeah, I'm good."

Mr. Weinstein interrupted and asked, "Did you tell them anything?"

"No. Of course not. There isn't anything for me to tell them, for one. And for two, you weren't present."

"Give me an hour and I'm going to find out what it is that they need to speak with you about. When I find out, of course I'm going to need you to be as honest with me so that I can know how I can defend you and make sure that you aren't, if they have any kind of evidence, spending time in jail, or prison. Go home and get something to eat and wait for my call," Weinstein explained. He turned and walked out of the police station with Reign and the fellas following behind him.

The ride back to their house was quiet, each with their own thoughts. Reign, although, she knew that they had nothing on her but it still didn't leave a good feeling over her. She needed to speak with Jameson. He had connections with the NYPD and she knew that he could get her the answers she needed. They arrived back at the house and Jackie had the door open waiting on them.

"What the hell was that all about? Is everything okay?" Jackie asked as they walked past her one by one.

"They just wanted to ask me about Pearl. What took Weinstein so long to get to me?" Reign asked calmly.

"When I spoke to him, he said that he was dealing with a client in Pennsylvania. What could they possibly want to know about Pearl that they don't already know?" Jackie asked.

"From what they said to me, the detective that was working on her case was killed. They came across his cases as they were cleaning out his office. Before Pearl…before I killed her, she had gone to him with concerns. Something about pinning me as being the Lipstick Killah. When they saw that, they decided that it would be best if they re-opened her case and started looking into the things that she had said. They were talking to each other and thought I didn't hear, but when they mentioned the Lipstick Killah, Williams had said that he had briefly heard about the quote, unquote, person. There was neither evidence nor suspects so the police department searching for this person was put on hold. That's just about what they told me. I have a feeling that this isn't going to be the end of this," Reign replied, pacing across the living room floor.

"Did you kill the cop that was working her case?" Senaj asked as everyone's attention diverted to him and he realized that the question was actually spoken.

"I don't go around killing people," Reign responded with an eye roll.

"I didn't mean it like that, Reign. I don't even know why I said that. It just spewed out and I apologize."

"Yeah, I'm sure."

"Reign, don't be like that," Senaj persisted, moving in her direction.

"I have to go see Jameson."

"We'll go with you," Jamori offered. He was talking about himself and Akuchi.

"You have to wait for Mr. Weinstein's phone call." Senaj sighed. He didn't want her to go see him or deal with him any longer.

"He has my cell phone number. He could reach me there. I'm sure that it's going to take Weinstein longer than an hour to find out what I need to know," Reign stated. She grabbed the car keys and left with Jamori and Akuchi behind her.

When they were gone, Senaj sank into the couch, defeated.

"She's grown, Senaj. You could talk to her until she blue in the face. She gonna do what she wants too and you're just going to have to let her do it." Jackie spoke the obvious and took a seat on the couch opposite of him.

"I know and that's what's upsetting me. I'm her man, I'm supposed to be protecting her. It feels like I'm just in her shadow and she's the one doing the protecting."

"I know. She's been playing but her own rules since her dad passed. It's what she's used to and doesn't know how to fully submit to a man. Just give her some time," Jackie said. She liked Senaj. In fact, she loved him as if he was her brother, but she didn't like how he allowed Reign to walk all over him. If they were going to make it, he was going to have to get a backbone soon.

***

Ding! Ding! Ding!

Reign laid her finger on Jameson's doorbell as if she was angry with the bell. Moments passed before Jameson came to the door. He looked at Reign with a twisted look until he noticed Jamori and Akuchi, two brolic dudes he'd never seen before, and his look disappeared.

"Reign? What are you doing here?" Jameson asked.

"We need to talk," she simply said with her hands on her waist.

"Now isn't a good time, Reign. Hit me up in the morning, and we can set a time later in the day."

Reign stepped in his direction, causing him to move back. Akuchi was the last one who came inside, so he closed and locked the door behind himself.

Reign said, "Right now is going to have to work just fine. There are somethings that I need to find out. Things that you should have been aware of."

"Things like what?" Jameson asked as he took a deep pull from a Cuban cigar.

"When I first agreed to come work for you, you guaranteed me that if my name would come up with NYPD, you would notify me. Correct?"

"Yeah."

"So why am I just getting back from them niggas over in 79th? They had me in there for hours, asking me questions about an old case in which I wasn't even a suspect in?"

"79th? An old case? About what?"

"My best friend was murdered. They said something about the case and the detective that was on it had notes about me. I'm still kind of foggy about it all. I need for you to find out."

"Find out what?" Jameson asked.

"Why they are targeting me to question? I gave my statement when she died. They should not be sniffing at my door."

Jameson put his cigar out and placed his hands at his side. He said, "I'm sure that it's nothing. They just want to cover all grounds. I can get back to you in a week."

"Three days," Reign stated. She meant it.

Without another word, she left his house. Something wasn't right. She didn't know what it was, but her gut was speaking loud and clear. She checked her cell to see if she just so happened to miss a call from Weinstein. She hadn't. Just like the ride there, the ride back was just as quiet. When they reached the house, Reign's phone rang. It was Weinstein.

"What you got for me?" Reign answered.

"We need to talk. I need you at my office first thing in the morning."

"Why can't we talk about it now?" Reign asked. She was eager to know what was going on, but she was also moving into her new house the next day.

"No. I don't want to speak on the phone."

"I'll be there at eight."

"Make it seven," Weinstein demanded.

Reign agreed and hung up the phone. Whatever it was that he needed to tell her, had to be serious. Could they connect her to the other murders that she had committed? What else could have Pearl said that she was causing drama even with her in the afterlife?

When they entered the house, Senaj jumped from the couch and looked at Reign.

"What happened?" he asked.

"I have to go see Weinstein in the morning."

"It's that bad you have to go in?"

"I don't know how bad it is until I get there. It looks like you and the fellas will have to do all the moving y'all selves. I need Jackie with me, just in case."

"A'ight. I'll see if Polite would be down with helping. What Jameson say?" Senaj asked, placing Reign's feet into his lap and massaging them.

Reign sighed. She didn't want to have to repeat what Jameson said. He didn't follow up with what it was he was supposed to do and wondered if he did know and didn't want to tell her anything, until he was sure. She said, "He claimed he didn't know. He said he would have something for me within a week. I didn't need a week, I need three days, and that's exactly what I told him."

"What if he doesn't get you the information that you need?"

Reign paused before she answered. She knew that her words were selected carefully as to not piss Senaj off. She responded, "We'll cross that bridge when we need too."

Senaj knew what she meant, but what was he supposed to do. He sighed and closed his eyes momentarily. When he opened them, he realized that he had dozed off. Everyone around him was packing and he sat confused slightly. Shaking off of his sleepiness, he got up and began to help them.

***

The next morning, Reign had gotten up early with a heavy heart and headed to Weinstein's office with Jackie. Jackie tried to reassure Reign that everything would be alright. On the surface, Reign showed that she was convinced by what Jackie was telling her, but deep down, she knew that everything was going to shit. Before going onto Weinstein's office, Jackie and Reign prayed that everything would be fine.

Senaj woke around nine o' clock and got his day started with a cup of coffee. Senaj texted Polite to see if he was up to helping them move. Answering within minutes, Polite agreed and told Senaj that he would be there in no more than a half an hour. Slowly, Jamori gotten himself up and then Akuchi.

"Y'all ready for today?" Senaj asked, placing mugs of coffee in front of both Akuchi and Jamori.

They looked at Senaj like he was crazy and proceeded to sip on their coffee. Once done with coffee and dressed for the day, they began to load the U-Haul truck with boxes and furniture. They were halfway to Glen Cove when Senaj's phone began to ring. The number that popped up on the screen was one he didn't recognize. He answered anyway, maybe it was Reign or Jackie with an update.

"Hello," he answered skeptically.

"Mr. Ademyemi, this is Ian Brandoff. Your lawyer. How are you?"

"I'm well, and yourself?"

"Not too bad. Listen, I know it's Saturday and you want to enjoy your day, trust me, I know, but I was calling about the lawsuit that I filed."

Senaj's eyebrow went up. Jamori, Akuchi, and Polite looked at him trying to figure out who could be on the other end of the phone. Senaj responded, "Yes. What about it?"

"I was wondering if you had any interest in settling this thing outside of court?"

Senaj didn't hesitate when he responded, "Absolutely not! The point isn't about the money to me. It's the simple fact that there are police officers who were sworn in to protect and serve out here killing black people."

"Now come on, Mr. Ademyemi, that is not true," Mr. Brandoff stated.

Senaj looked at the phone in utter disbelief. He spoke in an even tone so as to not allow Mr. Brandoff to get him agitated. He said, "Mr. Brandoff, why was it that you took my case if you don't believe that, that isn't true? You won my case against the police department and got the officer who shot me fired and jail time. You were in that courtroom making a voice for all of the young and old black men in America who have been gunned down by police or have suffered abuse from them. How can you tell me that it's not true?"

"The officer never got to serve jail time. The Grim Reaper came to collect his body not too long after we won that case. Mr. Ademyemi. It was just a simple question."

"A simple question that got you fired. I will be looking for a new lawyer and I wish that you would cooperate with him or her if they need any information from you."

With that, that was the end of the conversation Senaj would have with Mr. Brandoff. First thing Monday morning, he was looking for a new lawyer.

"What the fuck was that?" Akuchi asked once Senaj had hung up.

Senaj, for the rest of the ride, had told the feelings the foolery Brandoff was talking about.

This was exactly what was wrong with the world today. The majority of the people in the world that lack melanin saw nothing wrong with their "people in power" killing black people. Senaj would find a lawyer that was about the cause of making an example out of corrupt police officers and their departments.

Mimi

Chapter Fourteen

It had been hours since she had left home. She paced back and forth along the gritty, dirty floor, wondering what the fuck was going on. One minute she was being questioned by Mr. Weinstein and next, the feds were flanking the inside of his office, throwing her to the ground with their knees in her back as if she had a weapon on her, and arresting her. They were yelling so many things that she didn't know exactly why they were arresting. Everything went by in a blur that she barely heard Mr. Weinstein telling her that he was going to be following behind them to find out what was wrong. Jackie was pressed against one of the female agents with tears streaming from her eyes.

Dragging Reign by the arms to stand her up, they pulled her out of Weinstein's office and outside. People were scattered everywhere, wondering what was going on and, in this day, and age people rather take out phones and record and try to go viral. Which was the case here. There were few people around when they took her out of the building but as they had her hemmed up against the black escalade truck, it seemed like everybody from a five-block radius were outside recording what was going on.

Reign wanted to break down, but she knew that she had to stay strong and have faith in Weinstein. She prayed so hard that she thought she was drowning God with all of her prayers. She had no sense on time it was, she just knew that she had been stuck in the cell for hours.

Footsteps coming towards her cell halted her pacing. She stood with her hands folded across and her legs spread as she watched a female agent walk towards a desk and grab a chair and place it in front of the cell. She was pretty too. She was 5'7" with thick hips, dark, blemish free, smooth skin, long hair which was placed in a ponytail, and manicured fingernails. Her outfit was a little bit boring and lacked color, but Reign knew that this was her "uniform". She wore a blue windbreaker with the word FED displayed in yellow on the back.

"You might as well get comfortable. You're gonna be in this cell until at least Monday morning when we get you in front of a judge," she spoke. She had a manila folder in her hands and was pretty thick.

"Why am I in here?" Reign asked.

"You don't know?" The agent smiled.

"I wouldn't be asking if I did know," Reign replied with sarcasm.

"Well, first let me introduce myself. My name is Agent Linden. I will be overseeing this case. We have arrested you on seven counts of first-degree murder."

"What!" Reign expressed.

"Don't play coy with me, Reign. You know like I know why you got those charges. We have been watching you."

"I'm not talking without my lawyer."

"We don't expect you to. I just came down to let you know what you were being charged with. You will see that you see a judge Monday and make sure there is no bail for you. You have been a menace and furthermore, a danger. Get ready for an extended stay."

Reign dropped her arms to her sides and looked at Agent Linden with a smug look. She said, "I appreciate you coming to deliver the message."

Agent Linden chuckled as she dragged the chair back to the table. Before she exited the room, she said, "I will see to it that someone brings you something to eat, drink, and get you a phone call. Perhaps you can call your fiancé, or your children?"

"Bitch, if I wasn't in this cell and you didn't have a badge, I would beat your ass. Leave my children and fiancé out of this!" Reign yelled behind her back as she cackled leaving out of the door. Frustrated, Reign sat on the metal table that would equate to her bed for the next two nights. She cursed herself to think that she was going to continue doing what she was doing. If she was found guilty, she was getting life, or possibly even life. She should have listened to Senaj the first time.

***

Sweating and breathing heavy, Senaj and the fellas were almost done with moving everything in the house. They decided to take a break and head to get something to eat. After locking up, they googled a restaurant that was three minutes away, called House of Wings. Jamori ordered garlic parmesan wings with fries, Senaj had the lemon pepper wings and fries, Polite opted for the chicken tenders and fries, and Akuchi had a Philly cheesesteak with Cajun ranch wings. Stomachs growling, they took their food back to the house and stood around the island in the kitchen munching on their food.

"Did anyone hear from Jackie or Reign?" Senaj asked munching on his wings and looking down at his phone.

"Nah. Which is weird 'cause it's been hours since anyone of us has spoken to them." Akuchi stated checking his phone as well. Polite shook his head no as he had a mouth full of fries.

Jamori was scrolling on Facebook, checking to see if there were any messages from his sister or cousin. There was none. They all looked at each other and knew that something wasn't right. Simultaneously, their phones began to go off with notifications, and messages. Senaj's phone rung with a private number. He answered.

"Hello?" he questioned.

"Hey babe." It was Reign. Her voice was low but he knew it was her immediately.

"Babe? What's wrong? Why are you calling me from a private phone number?"

"The FEDS came and got me from Weinstein's. They talking about charging me with seven counts of first-degree murder and that they have been watching me. I haven't spoken to Weinstein or Jackie since it's happened. There was a female agent who came and spoke with me. She said that they would be holding me until Monday. They are gonna try and make sure that I don't get bail." Reign was sobbing now.

Akuchi turned his phone around and was showing Senaj a video of Reign being hemmed against a SUV being searched. Senaj's mouth dropped. He turned his attention back to Reign and said, "I'm going to call Weinstein to make sure that he is on top of this. What do you need me to do, babe?"

"I just need you to make sure that if I do get bail, you have the money together. All my information is inside a brown satchel that is inside of the brown trunk that has my name on it. I love you and I should have listened to you. I'm so fucking stupid."

"No, babe. Look, we gonna work it out. Me and the fellas bout to head back to the city and I will see if my parents can keep the kids for a little while longer."

Reign sniffled and said, "I love you, Senaj. No matter what. I have to go but if I get another chance to call you, I will. If not, I will send a message to you through Weinstein. Call him now, babe, and see what he talking. I also have money for him. It's all inside of that trunk."

"I got you, babe. I love you too," Senaj said, before the line went dead.

He couldn't believe what the fuck was going on. He placed his phone onto the countertop and ran his hand down his face.

Polite passed Senaj his phone so that he could watch the video of Reign being arrested. His heart broke into so many pieces and he immediately wished that there was something that he could have done to prevent this. He wished that she would have just listened to him and got out of the game when he asked her too.

"Ain't no need to beat yourself up about this, bro. We gonna do all we can to help her get out," Akuchi replied.

"Come on. We got to get back to the city," Senaj said.

They cleaned up their mess and got back inside of the U-Haul truck. The ride was silent providing the enough time for Senaj to think about how he was going to get Reign out of this situation.

Mimi

Chapter Fifteen
A week later

Reign's bail had been set at five hundred thousand dollars. The judge was being very lenient with her considering the fact that she was being charged with several counts of murder. But like most judges, he thought she didn't have any money. So instead of revoking her bail hearing, he set it at five hundred thousand to give her hope. She needed ten percent of that in order for her to get out of jail and that was just chump change to her. She just dropped half a million on her new home so she was pretty sure that the fifty thousand dollars wasn't going to make or break her.

Reign was booked and took through the process of being searched and transferred to be held inside of the Metropolitan Detention Center, MDC for short. For the first two days, she was tried by the other females. To a person that didn't know Reign, from appearance only, they figured that she was reserved and wasn't about putting that work in. One girl made that mistake of trying to step to her to take her food. Reign wasn't eating the nasty shit so if the girl really wanted it, she would have given it to her with no questions asked. Reign guessed that this girl had something to prove though, which is why she was pressing Reign. It was only when the girl placed her finger in Reign's face, just inches away from her nose, Reign snapped and within seconds, she had broken the girl finger. Reign got out of Dodge after that. Fifteen minutes passed and she was sure that the CO's should have been on their way by now, but no one came.

Thinking that she was out of the clear, later that night she laid in her bunk, almost asleep. She was placed in a dorm, so she shared the space with several other women and was left vulnerable. Reign was in that in-between space where she was still somewhat alert but then also close to dreamland when she heard the slightest movement that was too close to comfort. She cracked one eyelid open and looked around. She saw figures moving in her direction, speaking in hushed tones.

"I know y'all don't thin, y'all gonna jump on me while y'all think I'm sleeping," Reign said loud enough for them to hear once they were close enough.

The light footsteps that were coming her way halted and she sat up in bed. At the head of the pack was the chick whose finger she had broken and four other girls who obviously, in their spare time, were smelling the pissy part of her panties. Reign sat on her bunk and looked at the group of women who just stood there looking at her like she was crazy.

"Don't try it. I'm not the one who y'all need to be fucking with. I'm not what my appearance seems and I have more reach out of these walls then y'all think. I'm pretty sure that I will be leaving this place by the end of the week and I can assure all of you that whatever amount of time y'all got will be that much harder for you of y'all jump on me," Reign stated with malice dripping from her voice.

"You broke Shanice's finger," someone from the back spoke up.

"So, I had no right to defend myself from someone who is trying to intimidate me? You bitches got the game fucked up. What do you think is going to happen when you keep poking a bear? That motherfucker gonna attack you! Now if y'all don't want nothing, get the fuck on before I make it a problem for all of y'all," Reign stated and laid down. The nerve of these bitches. She only let them slide like that because she knew she wasn't going to be in there for long and she didn't want to give anybody any reason to keep her ass there longer than what she needed to be.

The day after, the word had already spread that Reign, the new girl, was nothing to fuck with. It turned Reign stomach when she saw all the women in the jail flocking to her. This was not what she wanted and she expressed so to the women. They didn't get it though. No matter how many times Reign asked them to fall back, they still were stuck to her outer bubble like glue.

"Mills!"

She heard her name being called on the seventh day. It was lights out and she didn't know why the fuck the CO was calling her name so damn hard.

"Yes," she answered, raising her head from off of the piece of tissue they called a cot.

"Get your things together and get up," he said roughly.

Reign's heart leaped into her chest. She was finally going home. She looked around and there was nothing that she wanted to take. She took her sheets from off of the notepad and folded them up and followed the CO to discharge.

It took them another hour to process her out and when she was done, they handed her a bag that had her belongings in it. She went to the bathroom and changed into the outfit that she was arrested in. When she was done, they escorted her to the exit and she couldn't move fast enough to get out of the door. The door slammed behind her and she paused to smell the night air. A smile came across her face and she knew that she had to do all that she could to make sure she didn't spend the rest of her life behind bars.

"Babe!" she heard Senaj calling her.

She looked in the direction where his voice came from and there he was. Standing in all of his chocolate glory. Without thought, she sprinted his way and ran into his arms. Senaj caught her and her legs wrapped around his waist as her face was buried into his neck.

"Oh my God, I missed you!" Reign said as she placed kisses on his neck.

"I missed you too, love," Senaj responded while squeezing her tight.

They let each other go and made their way to the car. Reign looked at the time and noticed that it was almost midnight.

"Where are the kids?" Reign asked.

"My parents brought them home earlier today. When I left, they were sleeping."

"Who are they with?"

"Jackie got them. She was pretty fucked up when the Feds came and got you."

"I know she was fucked up when I was being brought outside. I gotta talk to her."

Riding back to the house they used to share with everybody, Reign told Senaj what happened while she was locked up. She told him how she planned to beat the case because she didn't want to be in there ever again.

The house was quiet when they got there and Reign decided to wait on talking with Jackie. She headed to the shower to wash the week-long jail stench off of her. Reign couldn't contain when she was able to use her coconut body scrub and feel fresh. Senaj was laying on the air bed in his pajama pants when she came out wrapped in a towel.

"Did you happen to speak to Weinstein?" Reign asked.

"I did. He wants you to go see him tomorrow morning. I'll come down with you."

"Babe, you don't have to. I know that this is my mess that I need to get together and I don't want to have to drag you into this. I should have listened to you the first time. For the longest time I did things my own way and I realized that by not listening to what you were telling me and being stubborn, I put myself here. It wouldn't be right for me to drag you into this," Reign said as she moisturized her skin with cocoa butter.

"Look, babe - "

Reign dropped her towel and covered his mouth. She straddled his waist and said, "Not right now. We can talk about all of this tomorrow. I just want to feel you inside of me."

Reign looked Senaj in his eyes and he nodded his head. She uncovered his mouth and winded her hips onto him. His dick came alive in little time and she smiled. Reign moved off of him and pulled his pants off and stared at his thickness with hunger in her eyes. She was between his legs, watching it as it bobbed to the side. Her mouth watered as she stood up and made her way to the closet. In there was a box that she kept for when she wanted to be kinky. She made sure that this was the last thing that she would leave in the house before they had officially moved into their new one. Placing the box on the bed next to Senaj, she took out a cherry-flavored lubricant that was safe for consumption. After opening it, she poured some of it onto her hand and rubbed it together. Placing her hands onto his thickness, she watched as his eyes closed and he felt the sensation of her hands stroking him up and down.

Tucking her legs under her body, she got comfortable and placed him in her mouth while using one hand to stroke him. Her mouth was warm on his dick and extra wet due to the mixture of her spit and lubricant. Senaj's hips pumped as her grip tightened around the base of his dick. Using her free hand, she gently massaged his balls, causing him to grunt. Effortlessly, his dick slid down her throat and saliva dripped from the sides.

"Mmm. Damn, babe," Senaj moaned as he wrapped his hands in her hair.

She smiled on the inside because she loved when he commented on her head.

Her jaws tightened around him as her pace sped up. She now was using both her hands and doing so in a twisting motion. Senaj kept his hands planted on her head and pumped, disregarding that his dick was now touching her heart. Reign stopped abruptly and wiped the sides of her mouth. She never completely finished giving him head. She didn't want to risk him not being able to get it up again.

Reign got off of the bed and got on her hands and knees. She arched her back and poked her ass out and wiggled it for Senaj to come and get it. The air bed made unpleasant sounds as Senaj moved from the bed and got on his knees behind her. Using his hand, he placed it on his dick to rub the head of his dick on her clit. He used his free hand to smack her ass. It stung a little bit, but she allowed it. Besides, she'd been a bad girl.

His dick was slippery in his hand so he stopped playing around and entered her. Reign moaned, satisfied that she was now filled with his thickness. Senaj held onto her waist and as she began to throw it back on him. Senaj long stroked Reign causing her to throw her head to the side and moan out.

"Yes! Just like that!" Reign moaned.

Senaj's pace picked up and he reached around her waist to place his finger on her clit causing stimulation. Reign collapsed to the floor but Senaj laid on top of her and kept going.

"You wanted this, right?" Senaj whispered in her ear.

"Ooh yes!" she moaned.

"Cum on this dick and show me just how much you wanted this."

That she did, as if it was on command. Her juices flowed onto his dick, causing the room to fill with noises as if there was macaroni being stirred.

"Damn, babe. This shit leaking like a leaking faucet," Senaj retorted.

When she was done cumming, he took his dick out and laid on his back on the floor. Breathing heavy, she got up and stood over Senaj. Before she sat on his dick, she slid her fingers in between her slit and rubbed her clit in a circular motion. Using her free hand, she rubbed her nipple and then placed it into her mouth.

Senaj couldn't help himself and he began to stoke it. His dick throbbed in his hand. He needed to bust that nut in the worst way. Reign coated her fingers with her nut. Removing her hands from between her thighs, she licked her glaze from her fingers. With a smile on her face, she lowered her body down to his and sat on his stick. With her feet planted on the floor, she bounced on his dick while holding onto the back of her neck, her fingers interlocked together.

"Ooh, I'm gonna cum again!" Reign shouted.

"Wait for me. I'm gonna cum with you," Senaj said and moved his hips and pumped faster. He held onto her waist as he let his seeds go inside of her.

Thirty seconds later she was lying next to him with her leg thrown over his legs, her hand on his chest, and her head resting in the crook of his arm.

"Damn, that was phenomenal," Senaj stated, his eyes heavy with sleep.

"Mm hmm. Tomorrow after I see Weinstein, we'll be able to do that and more to christen our new house. In every room. Except for the kids' rooms."

"That's right." Even though he had agreed, he didn't know if he even wanted her there.

***

After Reign went to see Weinstein, her heart was heavy. He expressed how mad the judge was when he found out that she had bailed out. Besides that, Weinstein said that they had a hundred and eighty days to get the evidence that they needed in order to indict her. Then she would have to sit in jail and wait for trial if they were successful in getting the evidence. She wouldn't and couldn't let that happen.

When she left his office, she needed to clear her mind. She found herself driving to the cemetery. Her mother, father, and grandmother were laid to rest side by side. She sat in front of her father's grave. The tears immediately began to fall.

"I wish y'all were here. I don't know how to get out of this mess and leaving isn't an option for me. If I didn't have the kids, I would leave in a heartbeat, even if it would mean that both me and Senaj's hearts would be broken. Senaj doesn't deserve any of this," she cried. Her soul ached because she never had to face something like this and be put in the position to have to be in prison for the rest of her life. Seeing her kids would be at a bare minimum, Senaj could possibly be with someone else, and she could be forgotten. If she had the heart to do so, she would have ended her life. That would have been better than what she was dealing with now. But it all came down to Senaj and the kids. She made her bed, now she has to lie in it.

The sun was setting by the time she decided to leave the cemetery. Her phone kept going off with phone calls and texts from Senaj worried about her. As she at behind the wheel of her truck, she simply texted that she was okay and started her truck up to get to her next destination.

Ding! Ding! Ding!

Reign stared at the door in front of her. It felt like eternity as she followed the wood lines before someone came and opened the door.

"Reign? What are you doing here? I've been trying to get in touch with you," Jameson said in shock.

"I know. I've been locked up in MDC. Ain't you gonna let me in?" Reign asked with her head tilted to the side.

"Yeah, come in." He moved out of the way.

When she entered his house, she made her way to the living room and noticed there was food on the coffee table and ESPN was on the TV screen.

"Did I interrupt?"

"Naw. I was running the streets all damn day and before you came, I was only catching up with what my body been needing all day. I'm glad that you are here though. I need to speak with you about something. Have a seat."

Reign sat on the couch and watched as Jameson turned the TV off and took his seat on the love seat opposite of her. He looked at Reign and began, "I need you to do a job."

"Straight to the point, huh? Glad that I did come because I was coming to tell you that I was out."

Jameson paused for a moment and then chuckled. His chuckle turned into laughter. When he calmed down, he asked, "Out of what? Because if you are talking about what I think that you're talking about, you might as well forget it. There is a contract between us that needs to be fulfilled."

"Verbal."

"It's still a contract."

"Jameson, you know what I'm dealing with, but yet and still you want me to off somebody. I am facing life behind bars. I won't see my kids. You got me fucked up if you think I'm gonna go out here and add another count onto my long list of charges."

"We have a contract."

"What are you gonna do? Sue me? Take me to fucking court and tell the damn judge that we have a verbal contract together for me to go kill motherfuckers for you? Is you stupid or is you dumb? Because whether you like it or not, I'm out." Reign stood up to leave. She was done with this life and this conversation.

Before she walked away, Jameson threw a folder onto the coffee table, halting Reign's steps.

"Go ahead. You know you want to see what's inside of this folder," Jameson taunted with a smirk on his face.

Curiosity got the best of her and she lifted the folder from the table and took the papers out. Her mouth dropped when she saw the face on the papers.

"You're joking, right? Surely you don't want me to off a federal agent?" She looked at him like he was crazy.

"Taking care of the person who holds your life in their hands isn't a joke."

"With all of the charges that they are hitting me with, I will be the first person that they come to look for, with or without evidence. You tripping right now and like I said before, I'm out. And I'm definitely not about to kill a federal agent," Reign stated. She threw the papers onto the table and turned to leave. She had made it to the door when she felt him grab her arm.

"You've killed a cop. What makes a Fed different?" he asked through gritted teeth.

How the fuck does he know about that, but couldn't tell me about the damn NYPD coming to shake my world up? she thought. Instead of asking that, she said, "Jameson, I'm only going to ask you this – no, I'm gonna tell you this one time, and one time only. Let go of my arm."

"And I'm gonna tell you this one time only. You're not out until I tell you that you're out. Get your senses together and do what you got to do."

What was this man not getting? Reign smirked at him. In her mind, she gave him a warning. Now if anything happened, it would fall on him.

Without warning, Reign used her free arm to come back down on his forearm, freeing his hold on her, and then punching him in the nose. Jameson hands flew to his face. He checked to see if it was broken, his hands a crimson red.

"You bitch!" Jameson yelled and ran towards Reign.

She was trapped in the corner and she had to get out of it. When Jameson reached Reign, he was too worried about his nose and when he swung at her, she side-stepped him and got her ass from out of the corner.

"What is up with men not being able to accept it when a woman tells them no? No means no," she taunted. Her feet were planted and her hands were up guarding her face. If a fight was what he wanted, a fight was what he was going to get.

Jameson walked up to Reign and kicked her hard and fast in her stomach, causing her to fly back onto the couch, toppling it on her way down. Jameson smiled smugly when he thought Reign was down for the count. He walked over to where she was, but she was gone. As he looked up, he saw her hiding behind a pillar, holding a vase over her head. She smiled and smashed it on top of his head. He fell to the floor and Reign instantly climbed on top of him and rained blows to his sides as hard as she could. Under her knuckles, if they weren't broken, she damn sure cracked. Reign was winded and he wasn't attempting to fight back, so she got up and figured she would walk away now. Except Jameson had a change of heart as he grabbed her by the leg and yanked as hard as he could and brought her down with a loud thud!

For what seemed like hours, Reign lay on her back, trying to catch her breath. She was getting too old to be fighting anyone, let alone a grown-ass man.

Reign looked down at her feet to see where Jameson was. He was struggling to get on his feet. Reign had to get up before he did, but just the slightest movement of her head felt like the room was spinning.

Jameson was faster than what Reign thought and he made it to her within seconds. He punched her in the chest so hard the wind was knocked out of her and she heard ringing in her ears. He grabbed her by her shirt and tried to get her to stand up.

"You want to fight me like you a dude? Get your ass up and fight me like you got a set of balls between your legs!" he yelled, raining spittle on her face.

He pushed her against the dining room table, allowing her to get her second wind. Just as she was about to swing, he two pieced her, splitting her lip and opening the flood gates for her nose to leak like a faucet.

The sight of her own blood both excited and angered her. Reign's adrenaline pumped as she straightened herself and screamed while attacking him as if she had eight arms like an octopus. Every inch of his body was connected with her tiny but powerful fists. Jameson fell to his knees, trying to breathe and push Reign off of him. She had turned into a mad woman. With a swift kick to his face, teeth and blood flew from his mouth and fell over in slow motion like he was in a movie.

"Bitch, when I tell you I'm out, I mean that shit!" she yelled in between breaths.

She went into the kitchen to find a bottle of water somewhere. She located one at the bottom of the fridge. She opened the top and guzzled half of the bottle down in five seconds. She made her way back to the dining room and almost dropped her bottle of water when she noticed that he was gone. She walked towards the living room and got punched in the jaw and fell. Jameson climbed on top of Reign and wrapped his hands around her throat. She instantly grabbed at his hands to get him off of her, but it failed. She panicked. Prison was a better option than death. At least in prison, she would be able to see her kids. It was either flight or fight and she would always choose fight. Struggling to reach her lower back, she took one of her guns from her lower back and aimed it in his side.

"You should have just let me leave," she struggled to say and then she let it go.

His grip around her neck loosened as he slowly fell to the right of her. When his hands were free from her neck, she gasped for air. Her chest rising and falling rapidly. The last thing she wanted to do was kill another motherfucker. But in order to save herself, she had to do what she had to do. Reign got up from off of the floor and watched as a pool of blood formed under Jameson. On her way to his house, she had prepared for this. She had a feeling that he wasn't going to let her go easy and she always followed her gut. She placed her gun in its place and went out to her truck. She grabbed the itchy hotel blanket and went back inside.

Reign placed the blanket on the floor and rolled his body onto it. Jameson's bowels had mixed with his blood and the smell was turning her stomach. Reign folded the blanket over Jameson's body and dragged it to her truck. She was sweating and was starting to smell. With what little strength she had, she hoisted his body onto the back of her truck, onto the tarp that laid on the bottom of the trunk. Once he was inside, she used the sweater that she had on to wipe her face free from the blood that had leaked from her nose and mouth.

Reign climbed into the driver seat, throwing her sweater onto the passenger seat, and made her way to the New York Harbor. She made sure that she was extra careful so as to not alert the police to her vehicle. Once she made it to her destination, she drove to a secluded spot and dragged his body from the truck onto a huge boulder.

Reign left him momentarily to search for heavy rocks to place inside of his pants in order to make sure that he sunk to the bottom of the river. Upon her task being completed, she pushed his body off of the boulder and watched as the current took his body away. She stayed until she couldn't see his body anymore and kept her fingers crossed that the rocks worked.

***

It was damn near midnight when Reign made it to her old house. She sat in the driveway to get her bearings. She needed to get rid of her tuck and somehow get to Jameson's house to clean up his house. A thought popped into her head as she reached for her phone. Senaj called her several times after she had texted him that she was fine. She'd speak to him when she got inside of the house.

"Hello? Reign, where the fuck have you been? This nigga in here losing his shit," Jamori stated.

"I know, I could tell by the missed phone calls. After I saw Weinstein, I had to clear my mind so I went to go visit my mama, daddy, and Nana. Can you come outside right quick? Don't tell Senaj."

"How long have you been outside?"

"Not long. I need to talk to you about something."

"A'ight. I'm coming."

As soon as Reign hung up, she had gotten a text from Senaj letting her know that he knew that she was outside. Responding, she told him to give her a minute and they would talk when she got inside. When she was done sending the text, she looked up to see Jamori was bouncing his way down the stairs. That was her cue for her to get out of the truck.

"Well, don't you look like shit? You haven't looked in the mirror today?" Jamori stated with a chuckle.

"It's not the time to laugh. I need a favor from you."

"What's up?"

"You think you could get a few of your people to go out somewhere to clean something up and burn my truck."

Jamori rubbed his hand down his face and asked, "What happened?"

"I went to tell Jameson that I was out. He didn't see it my way, so we fought to death. He lost and is literally sleeping with the fishes. Tell your boys they'll get three G's each when the job is done."

"I got you. Go in there before that boy has a heart attack," Jamori stated and gave her a hug. He didn't know how bad she needed it.

Reign looked up at the house and exhaled. It was time for her to face the drama.

Mimi

Chapter Fifteen

Senaj was waiting in the living room for Reign when she walked in. When he caught sight of her, he didn't know whether to hug her or curse her out. She looked like she had been through a war, with her hair all over her head, her face was swollen two times the normal size, and there was dried-up blood caked up on parts of her face. When he last seen her that morning, she definitely didn't look like that. Reign avoided eye contact with him but his stare was burning a hole in her.

"You just gonna sit there looking stupid, or you gonna tell me where the fuck you disappeared to all fucking day?" Senaj asked. He was pissed off to the max and didn't know if this time he would be able to contain it. Reign didn't want to explain anything to him, but she knew she had too.

"After I went to see Weinstein, I went to go see my parents and Nana." She paused. His demeanor softened, so she continued, "My heart and mind were so heavy, I just needed some place quiet to think, to vent for just a moment, without anyone passing judgement on me. After I left the cemetery, I went to Jameson's."

"What the fuck for?" Senaj asked, ready to explode.

"To let him know that I was out. That I had too much shit riding for me to stay free. That my family meant way more to me than any amount of money. But he didn't want to hear it." Reign hiccupped. She realized that she was crying.

"What do you mean he didn't want to let you?"

"I was leaving and he presented me with a folder. He wanted me to do another job, even after I told him I was out. I opened the folder and thinking back on it, I shouldn't have, but I did, and it was my mistake. The picture on the paper was the female agent that came and talked to me in the holding cell. I told him he was crazy and tried to leave again and when I got to the door, he tried to stop me by putting his hand on my arm. He didn't let go when I asked him to so we started fighting. That's why my face looks like this." Reign exhaled. She was relieved that she had let everything out. She'd been crying so hard.

Senaj walked up to Reign and lifted her head by her chin. He searched her face and could absolutely agree that her face was pretty banged up. There was blood caked up on the sides of her nose and in the corners of her mouth.

"What happened after y'all fought?" Senaj asked while looking intensely in her eyes.

"He was on top of me, choking me. I couldn't breathe and I wanted him off of me. I shot him."

"You what?"

"I killed him. I needed to get him off of me. I'd rather be alive dealing with the shit with the Feds than die by his hands. I had to do what I had to do." Reign placed her hands over her face and cried into them.

As badly as he wanted to be angry with her, seeing her cry did something to him. He wrapped his arms around her and held her tight. The world seemed right in his arms. "It's going to be okay," he said, rubbing her back softly.

"I just don't know what I'm gonna do. If I spend the rest of my life in prison, you're going to move on, I will barely get to see the kids, and they are going to hate me for not being there. Why didn't I just listen to you?"

"Shh! It's gonna be okay. We'll deal with that if we have to. Reign, I love you with everything in my body. I'm not going nowhere. I'm gonna ride this out with you. I'm mad as hell and I have every right to be. But I can't let that overtake me because I know I gotta be there for you and the kids. There is nothing that we can do to change what has happened, only what is going to head our way. I will make sure the kids understand and don't form a hatred for you. I will make sure that they come and visit every chance that we can. We don't even know for sure if you are going to spend any time in prison. Let's not speak that into existence. But God forbid it does, babe, I will hold you down."

Reign settled down quite a bit after she heard the promises that he made. She knew that Senaj would keep his promises and everything would be okay. Or so she hoped.

"Thank you," Reign murmured against his chest.

"For what?"

"Everything. You were sent to me for a reason and I was too stupid, stubborn, and blind to see that. God made sure to bless me with you, but I didn't see that he sent you to save me from myself. I'm sorry, and I don't know if I could say it more than I already have."

Senaj kissed the top of her head and replied, "Stop apologizing. Let's go get you cleaned up. Where did Jamori go?"

"I needed him to round up some of his boys to go clean up."

Senaj nodded his head and grabbed Reign's hand to pull her upstairs. Once there, Senaj ran Reign a hot bubble bath and helped her with taking her clothes off. He noticed the black and blue bruises that lined her rib cage and her legs. The bruise on her back was something that you only see in movies, never in real life. Reign lowered herself into the tub and winced at the pain that rocked her body. When her body was submerged into the water, Senaj took a seat on the closed toilet seat.

"Babe, why don't you just go to bed? You have to be to work in the morning."

"I took a leave of absence. I explained to my administrative that I had a family emergency. Of course, they don't know what kind, but she didn't ask any additional questions. All she simply sad was that she understood because she has a family. She wished me the best and told me to handle what I needed to handle."

Reign shook her head and said, "No, Senaj. That's not fair to you. I wouldn't want you to stop doing what you love on account of me."

"What's done is done, Reign, and ain't no coming back from it until I get ready to."

Reign exhaled and decided to let the situation be. She didn't want to argue. She was in pain and the hot water against her body felt heavenly. She closed her eyes and leaned against the back of the tub to relax.

Seconds later, Senaj told her that he was going to heat her up some food. He'd heard her stomach growling and only could imagine how hungry she was, going all day without eating. In reality, he needed to get away. He meant what he said to Reign because he loved and care for her and she had every right to defend herself. The thing is that, if she didn't go up there to begin with then she wouldn't have had to defend herself.

While he was heating up some leftover rice and beans and fried chicken, Jamori came inside of the house. He looked kind of spooked and was pacing back and forth around the living room. Senaj came out of the kitchen and appeared into the living room.

"Everything okay?" he asked.

"Nah, bro."

"What happened?"

"Where's Reign?"

"In the tub. What's up?"

"Did she tell you what was going on?" Jamori asked. If she didn't, he didn't want to be the one to over step that boundary and tell him.

"Yeah, I know."

Jamori paced some more, going back and forth with himself as to whether or not he should tell Senaj what was going on. The microwave went off so Senaj went to go grab the food, returning with a hot plate of food. He waited for Jamori to begin.

"I rounded up some dudes to go clean up the mess at Jameson's and one of my boys noticed cameras in the living room and the kitchen. We searched his entire house and couldn't find out where he was hiding the footage. We then began to tear out all of the camera's we saw and snipped the wires. If someone were to come check on him, she's not only going to go down for his murder, but me and my boys going to go down as accomplices. That's if they find out where he keeps the footage," Jamori panicked.

"I'm sure no one is going to go check up on that dude," Senaj stated and made his way to go upstairs.

"Senaj, you don't understand. You're not in this life. Anything is possible. That man is somebody's son, brother, man, nephew, uncle, or cousin. If the person he speaks to on a daily don't hear from him, they are bound to come and check on him."

"I may not be in that life, but I understand most things. From what I know of him, he's a pretty lonely man. I did a background check on him a while ago. All of his older family members are dead, aunts, uncles, and cousins are on the west coast. He has no siblings or a spouse. The only person that he could have been talking to every day would be his street soldiers."

"I need to talk to Reign," Jamori stated.

Senaj wanted to laugh at him. His movements were comical to Senaj, but he managed to keep his composure.

"Can it wait until the morning? It's already late and she's pretty banged up. I just want her to eat and get some rest."

As much as Jamori knew that it was right to talk with Reign, he knew the right thing to do was let her rest. She had been through hell. Rubbing his hand down his face, he replied, "Yes, it can wait. Just tell her to come talk to me as soon as she gets up in the morning."

"I got you. We going to the new house tomorrow so I'll make sure that she talks to you before we leave."

"A'ight. Thanks, bro," Jamori said and walked away to his room.

Senaj exhaled and made his way upstairs. Opening the door, Reign was passed out int the bed with the towel wrapped around her like a sheet. Turning back around, he went back to the kitchen to warp her food up and put it in the fridge. Before going back to their room, he checked the kids and then called it a night.

***

Reign was up at five o' clock in the morning. Zariyah was screaming her head off through the baby monitor and Senaj was knocked out, dead to the world. Rolling out of the bed, she put on a shirt and sweatpants to go to the kids' room. She lifted Zariyah into her arms and pressed her close to her body. Zariyah instantly settled down as Reign rocked her from side to side. She kissed the top of her head and made her way downstairs to heat up a bottle for her. As she continued to rock her, she couldn't help the tears that fell down her face.

"You are the most perfect gift that I have ever received in this fucked-up life I lived. You don't understand now, and I just hope that when you are old enough, you know how much I love you and Kahlil. I hope that your daddy tells you every day that I love you," Reign whispered in her ear. She wiped her tears and grabbed Zariyah's bottle from the bottle warmer, testing the milk against her wrist. Satisfied that the milk was the right temperature, she walked into the living room to get comfortable.

"Cuz?" Jamori asked. He had woken up because he had heard Reign moving around. In his panicked state, he thought she was an intruder.

"Yeah?" she replied.

He exhaled and said, "Girl, your whole head was about to be splattered across this floor."

Reign watched as he walked into the living and sit next to her on the couch. She said, "Zariyah was screaming bloody murder."

"Really? I must have been knocked out. I only heard you moving around. I'm gonna go put on some coffee. You want some?"

"Yeah. I could use some. I know that I'm gonna be up for the rest of the day. Thanks."

"No problem." Jamori went to the kitchen, put the coffee, and returned back into the living within five minutes. He sat back down on the couch wondering how he was going to bring up the camera situation.

"How's everything with Tina?" Reign asked, taking him from his current thoughts.

"Good, surprisingly."

"Why surprisingly?" Reign laughed.

"Because my trust issues are all fucked up and I'm trying to correct them, but Tina is patient. I know that I love her, but I'm not so sure that I am in love with her."

"Don't try so hard. Let it happen. If she is patient with your hard-headed ass now, she will be patient with you forever."

"I don't want to be that person, that's wakes up one day and she's gone. I don't want to dwell on the should of, could of, would of's."

"You show her that you love her every day. Talk to her. Always be open and honest with her, even if it means that it has to hurt. You'll get there and Jamori let me tell you, it's nothing in this world that could compare to true love. When you feel it, you'll think how your heart is with Tina, and compare it to what it felt like with ole girl that slept with you friend, and you're gonna ask yourself, what the fuck was I thinking."

Jamori laughed. He watched the smile on Reign's face about being in love and he knew that it was genuine. He said, "True, true. Listen, Reign, I want to talk to you about something."

Zariyah was done eating. Reign placed her on her shoulder to burp her. Reign looked at Jamori and asked, "What's up? Everything good?"

"If I'm going to be honest, then no, everything ain't good. One of my boys found cameras in Jameson's house. When he made the discovery, we began to search the house to find the feed. We couldn't find it. So we snatched what cameras we saw from the walls and cutting the wires." Jamori finally spoke about what was weighting heavy on his heart.

"Why didn't you tell me last night?"

"I wanted to, but Senaj told me to let you rest."

"Who does he think he is?" Reign seethed.

"Naw, don't do that. You were in pretty bad shape. He was just looking out for you."

Reign shook her head and said, "If only I knew last night, we could have gotten a head start in things. Jameson wouldn't have had the TV's in plain sight. I could only imagine that they in the walls. You think you and your boys could go back out there and see what's up? If y'all have to knock walls down, then do so."

"Yeah, we got you. Senaj did mention that y'all were going to y'all's house today."

"Yep. I love y'all but I need to get away and have some peace and quiet."

"I understand. Soon it's going to be just Akuchi and Jackie in here."

"You leaving?" Reign questioned.

"Yeah, at some point I will."

"With Tina?"

Jamori couldn't help but smile. He said, "Maybe. This ain't about me though. Let me get these niggas up though so we can get this shit done."

"I can't thank you enough. When you're done come to the house to get y'all money."

"You got it." Jamori got up and kissed both Reign and Zariyah on the top of their heads and left the room.

Zariyah was back to sleep and Reign brought her upstairs to change her and lay her down. Reign went inside of the room that she had shared with Senaj. She looked down upon his face and wanted to wake him with a slap to the face due to him not allowing Jamori to let her know about the mishap they ran into. Instead, she woke him up so they could pack what was left into Senaj's car and go home.

Mimi

Chapter Sixteen
Four Days Later

Bang! Bang! Bang!

Jackie stirred in her sleep. She was dreaming of simpler times when it was just her, Jamori, and Nana. There was a banging off in the distance that wouldn't stop. Next to her, Akuchi was laying silently. As if he couldn't hear the banging. The banging was getting louder, jolting Jackie up right. She looked around the room, startled as she listened to the banging.

"Akuchi," she whispered.

"Huh?" Akuchi murmured, still with his eyes closed.

"Come on, get up. I don't know if Jamori hears the door or not, but somebody is trying to knock the damn door down," Jackie panicked. The banging continued and she rocked Akuchi until he was fully awake and climbing out of the bed.

"Okay, I'm up," he said. In his basketball shorts, he made his way down the stairs with Jackie following him.

When they got to the door, Akuchi swung it open and was greeted with yelling police officers. They instantly threw their hands in the air, only that wasn't enough. The officers at the door forced Akuchi and Jackie to the ground and the remaining officers piled into the house. Akuchi and Jackie heard them yelling clear with every room that they had entered. When they got to Jamori's room, they yelled for him and Tina to get up and get into the living room. Akuchi and Jackie were now in the living room sitting on the couch. Jackie sat stoned faced, ever since Reign was bombarded and handled like she was shit on the bottom of a shoe. She didn't particularly like the police. They were everywhere, tossing shit all over the place for absolutely no reason.

"Can someone tell me what this is about?" Jackie asked, looking at all of the male officers dressed in tactical wear.

No one said anything. A female came through the crowd, took a seat on the coffee table, and looked at Jackie.

"I'm Agent Linden." She turned and pointed to the male that made his way across the living room. She continued, "That's my partner, Agent Mickens, and we are with the FBI. We would appreciate it if you fully cooperate with us. There are a few things that we need to know and the first is, where is your cousin Reign?"

Jackie looked directly in the agent's eyes and responded, "I don't know."

Agent Linden smirked and said, "So the empty bedroom upstairs, you didn't notice? She's out on bail. Did she go to another country? Where is she?"

"I don't know where she is. All I know us that she and her fiancé were packing things to move to his parents' house just in case she was going to be going to prison. Hell, they could be at any hotel in this damn city and I wouldn't even know. If my cousin did something wrong and she's found guilty, she's gonna take her punishment. But I doubt that she would run or that she did anything wrong, for that matter. I am aware that she doesn't have a court date so I ask again, what is this about and I will make sure that she gets the message."

"You're so smart. Not that it's any of your business, but I'll amuse you. Your cousin was working under a federal agent who took his undercover work too seriously and started living the life that we provided for him to be undercover. Now he's dead and we have footage of his murder. If you know where she is, give me a call. Or better yet, have her turn herself in. It'll be better if she did. Until then, he's coming with us," Agent Linden stated, turning to Jamori.

His head hung low as officers pulled him up from the couch and placed him in hand cuffs. They began to read him his rights.

"What is he under arrest for? He didn't do anything!" Jackie yelled as she jumped from the couch.

The sun had begun to surface and Tina sat on the couch in tears. Just the other day he was telling her what happened at Jameson's and that there was a possibility that he could go to jail. She promised that she would be by his side because she loved him that much. Of course, she didn't know how she was going to juggle going to school, working, and going to visit Jamori. But she would do it.

"He was involved with the cleanup. If you mention we got him, she might turn herself in sooner than what we want her too."

"No! You can't take him away from me!" Jackie screamed, tears cascading down her face.

They ignored her as they began to file out of the house on by one. Akuchi's heart broke seeing Jackie break down the way she did. He's never seen her this distraught and he didn't know what to do except hold her.

Tina left the living room to put on some proper clothes. "I'm going to follow them. Y'all coming?" she asked on her way out the door.

Jackie was on the floor next to the couch, holding onto Akuchi's leg. She couldn't respond.

"Nah, Tina. We'll catch up. Call us and let us know something. I'm gonna get Weinstein on the phone and get Jackie together."

"Okay. Be waiting for my call."

Tina ran out of the house, slamming the door behind her. Akuchi sank to the floor and wrapped his arms around his wife. Besides Reign and Kahlil, Jamori was the only blood that she had left.

"It's going to be okay," he said softly.

No matter what he said, she believed none of it. Ten minutes in her crying fit, she stopped suddenly and tried catching her breath. "I can't believe this shit," she said, sitting up.

"Are getting ready to go see Jamori?" Akuchi asked, getting up from the floor with Jackie.

"Nah. Tina can handle it herself for now. If she needs anything, she'll call me." Jackie was like a madwoman, now in the bedroom throwing clothes around the place.

"So, where you 'bout to go?" Akuchi was so confused but as her husband, whatever she was getting ready to do, he was about to do it with her. "

"I'm 'bout to go give Reign this ass whopping."

"Whoa! That's your family, babe. You can't do that," Akuchi said while slowing his pace.

"I can and I will. Reign has been my family for two and a half minutes. Jamori been my family my whole life. He is my twin, for God's sake! She dragged him into this bullshit and it ain't fair that he's sitting in that damn jail cell and she not. So, are you coming or not?" Jackie stated with her hands on her hips.

Akuchi knew she meant business and he hated to be in this situation. Senaj was his only brother and he didn't know what type of drama it would bring between them. After all, he would have to side with his wife. Both he and Jackie were in the blind about the reason why Jameson was killed and why Reign had done it, not to mention that Jamori dumb ass had helped her clean it up.

Jackie's hands were still on her hips and she was awaiting his response. He weighed the pros and cons of the situation and the only thing that he came up with was that he was riding with his wife. He nodded his head and continued to get dressed. He knew this would not end well.

***

The sun was beaming in on Senaj and Reign, causing Senaj to awake from his slumber, squinting his eyes. Reign was facing the opposite direction, snoring lightly. The smile on Senaj's face couldn't be contained. He was ecstatic that he was now in his own home with his kids and fiancée. He wished that this moment would last forever. He reached to the floor for his phone to check the time but a text message from his brother, that was sent almost an hour ago, caught his attention.

Akuchi: Bro, we got a situation!

He texted back, asking what had happened, confused as to what could have possibly gone wrong.

Banging on his door deterred his attention from his phone and he watched as Reign jumped up from her sleep, retrieving a gun from under her pillow.

"Put that away," Senaj glared. He got up from the bed and put sweatpants on to find out who it was banging on the door so early in the morning. He made his way down the stairs and could distinctly make out a female voice yelling. He was beyond confused, only family knew where they lived. As he got closer to the door, he recognized the voice to be Jackie's.

"Reign! Where the fuck you at? Come on, open this damn door now!" she yelled.

Senaj rushed to the door and opened it in bewilderment. He asked, "What the fuck is going on?"

"Senaj, you better move out of my damn way! My beef isn't with you! It's with my bum-ass cousin!" Jackie yelled.

Senaj looked at his brother, wondering what was going on. Jackie pushed her way into the house and Akuchi followed.

"Could y'all tell me what the fuck is going on?"

"Reign! I'd hate to have to come find you! Come downstairs!"

Senaj looked at Akuchi for answers, but his brother stayed tight-lipped. Reign appeared at the top of the stairs tying her sash on her robe, looking just as confused as Senaj.

"Jackie, what's going on? And why are you yelling?"

"My brother is locked up is what's going on!"

"What?" Reign questioned.

As soon as her foot touched the last stair on the landing, Jackie rocked Reign in her face, causing her to stumble back onto the stairs. Senaj's mouth dropped and watched as Jackie grabbed Reign by her robe to pick her back up.

"Bitch, you got my brother locked up behind your dumb ass! I'm finna beat your ass!"

When Reign realized what was going on, fight came into play and Reign knew what time it was. Reign knocked Jackie's hands away from her and two-pieced Jackie, followed by a jab to the stomach. Jackie fell to the floor and Reign waited for Jackie to get up. Reign wouldn't fight her while she was down. That was too dirty, even for her.

"You want to fight? Get the fuck up! I never asked Jamori to step foot into that house! I only asked him to gather up his boys. They weren't supposed to enter that house! Him getting locked up is on him and not me!" Reign spat angrily.

Senaj finally realized what was going on. He looked at his brother, who stood there with his hands in his pockets, not saying a word.

Jackie managed to gather herself from the floor and to her feet. Guarding her face, she swung at Reign, making the connection to the chin. Reign stumbled a tad bit, but she recovered quickly and jabbed Jackie in the stomach, causing her face to be left open and giving Reign the window to deliver a mean right hook. In the middle of the living room floor, they went at it as if they had been trained to fight by Mike Tyson himself.

"Bro, you not gonna get your wife?" Senaj asked.

"I'm not doing nothing. They gonna tire themselves out. Let them get this shit out of the way," Akuchi responded.

Two minutes in they were breathing heavy and tired, but neither wanted to give in.

Jackie yelled, "You came into our lives and turned everything upside down! I fucking lied for you when they asked me where you were, not thinking that they were going to be locking up the only family that I have left! You a cold bitch, Reign, and I hope they give your ass life behind all the bullshit you caused!"

At this point, they had stopped swinging and were now both pacing back and forth in the living room, crying. Reign knew she wasn't responsible for Jamori getting locked up, but she knew trying to get Jackie to understand that would be like talking to a brick wall.

Reign placed her hands on her hips and said, "I didn't tell him to go in there, Jackie. I would have never sent him in there knowing that I had done killed somebody. I may be a cold bitch, Jackie, but I know what the fuck I was doing by telling him to get his boys in there. Him getting arrested isn't on me, whether you like it or not."

"Fuck you! You're dead to me, bitch! I don't even know why my grandmother let you in. You came and fucked everything up. Senaj, good luck with this bitch! She will be behind bars and still won't allow you to be a man. You will always be her puppy!" Jackie yelled. She wanted everybody in that room to hurt the way she was - all except Akuchi. She washed her hands of Reign. She would help her brother out with a lawyer that she would pay for. When she said that Reign was dead to her, she meant it. As she turned her back to walk out of the house, she forgot to let Reign know one little detail. She stared at Reign, wishing she'd drop dead right there, and said, "If you weren't sure that you were going to prison for the rest of your life, maybe you should rethink that. Ya boy Jameson was a Fed."

Reign's heart pounded in her chest. The smirk that arose on Jackie's face pitched fire deep within Reign and Reign saw red. She ran in Jackie's direction, screaming from deep within, and grabbed her with one hand. She used her fist to rain blows to her face, causing Jackie's face to open up and bleed. They began to tussle and the next thing Senaj and Akuchi knew, they were falling through the big bay window and onto the lawn.

Reign was going for blood and choking Jackie by the time the two brothers got outside. They had finally seen enough. Both Jackie and Reign were bloody and bruised. Senaj grabbed Reign from off top of Jackie and dragged her into the house, all the while yelling obscenities. Once he made sure she was in there, he went out to go make sure that Jackie was okay, but Akuchi had already placed her in the car and they were backing out of the driveway.

"This is about some bullshit!" Senaj said to himself. He threw his hands up and made his way back into the house. Shit had truly hit the fan.

Chapter Seventeen

What's done in the dark will always come to the light. I've always lived my life with an "I don't care" attitude. I was raised as an only child so for me, everything was thrown at me and I always felt like I was that bitch. I never had to bow down to anyone. They bowed down to me. But life has a funny way of teaching you lessons. I never realized how fucked up I treated the people around me and never knew that they never told me no.

When I found out that Jamori had gotten locked up, my heart broke. Granted, I didn't tell him to go into that house, but I felt that I was responsible because just as easy as I asked him to get his people, I could have done the same thing. So in hindsight, Jackie was right. It was my fault that he was locked up. Behind my ass, he is spending five years in a maximum-security prison. Everything that I tried to do to help, Jackie turned it down. I couldn't blame her.

Senaj, my blessing, has been by my side through everything. When they sentenced me to twenty-five to life, I knew it broke his heart. From the moment that I turned myself into the Feds until the day they found my ass guilty, he was right by my side. He truly loved me and I couldn't repay him with having to stick by my side through this bid. There was no way in hell that even after I served twenty-five years they would they let me out. The first six months I spent in prison, I went back and forth with myself about a decision that I knew that I had to make. In a letter that I had written to Senaj, the love of my life, I told him not to wait for me. That he was free to move on. The only thing that I wanted him to do was write me every month with updates and pictures of the kids and for him to bring them for visits whenever he could.

In return, he sent me a packet that he had gotten from NYSDOC Bare Hill Correctional Facility to get permission granted for us to get married. He completed most of the paperwork but of course, he needed my signature. When I received it, I cried so many tears. I didn't deserve this man. It took me a month to sign the papers and send them back. Of course I'd marry him, even if I had done told him that he was free to do whatever it is that he wanted to do. He has shown me real love, so why not grant him that?

If I knew then what I knew now, I would have listened to Senaj. This prison shit is for the birds and I had to get accustomed to this shit. After all, this was the bed that I chose to lie in. Many nights I've lain awake thinking about what could happen if I was let out. My life would be so much different and I would do everything in my power to make sure that I changed and become a better person. That's wishful thinking though. Through this all, I can admit and say this was an eye opener for sure and a lesson learned.

The one thing that I am proud of and one thing that I wouldn't change is the fact that even if I don't get out, I know that my future husband and our children are set for life. They ain't never gonna go broke or hungry. Knowing that they good, I will never feel remorseful for being able to do that for them!

The End!

Submission Guideline

Submit the first three chapters of your completed manuscript to ldpsubmissions@gmail.com, subject line: Your book's title. The manuscript must be in a .doc file and sent as an attachment. Document should be in Times New Roman, double spaced and in size 12 font. Also, provide your synopsis and full contact information. If sending multiple submissions, they must each be in a separate email.

Have a story but no way to send it electronically? You can still submit to LDP/Ca$h Presents. Send in the first three chapters, written or typed, of your completed manuscript to:

LDP: Submissions Dept
Po Box 870494
Mesquite, Tx 75187

DO NOT send original manuscript. Must be a duplicate.

Provide your synopsis and a cover letter containing your full contact information.

Thanks for considering LDP and Ca$h Presents.

BOW DOWN TO MY GANGSTA

By **Ca$h**

TORN BETWEEN TWO

By **Coffee**

BLOOD STAINS OF A SHOTTA **III**

By **Jamaica**

STEADY MOBBIN **III**

By **Marcellus Allen**

BLOOD OF A BOSS **VI**

By **Askari**

LOYAL TO THE GAME **IV**

LIFE OF SIN II

By **T.J. & Jelissa**

A DOPEBOY'S PRAYER **II**

By **Eddie "Wolf" Lee**

IF LOVING YOU IS WRONG… **III**

LOVE ME EVEN WHEN IT HURTS **III**

By **Jelissa**

TRUE SAVAGE **VII**

By **Chris Green**

BLAST FOR ME **III**

DUFFLE BAG CARTEL III

By **Ghost**

ADDICTIED TO THE DRAMA **III**

By **Jamila Mathis**

A HUSTLER'S DECEIT 3

KILL ZONE **II**

BAE BELONGS TO ME III

SOUL OF A MONSTER

By **Aryanna**

THE COST OF LOYALTY **III**

By **Kweli**

SHE FELL IN LOVE WITH A REAL ONE **II**

By **Tamara Butler**

RENEGADE BOYS **III**

By **Meesha**

CORRUPTED BY A GANGSTA **IV**

By **Destiny Skai**

A GANGSTER'S CODE **III**

By **J-Blunt**

KING OF NEW YORK V

RISE TO POWER III

COKE KINGS II

By **T.J. Edwards**

GORILLAZ IN THE BAY III

De'Kari

THE STREETS ARE CALLING II

Duquie Wilson

KINGPIN KILLAZ IV

STREET KINGS 2

PAID IN BLOOD 2

Hood Rich

Mimi

STEADY MOBBIN' **III**
Marcellus Allen
SINS OF A HUSTLA II
ASAD
TRIGGADALE II
Elijah R. Freeman
MARRIED TO A BOSS III
By Destiny Skai & Chris Green
KINGS OF THE GAME III
Playa Ray

<u>**Available Now**</u>
<u>RESTRAINING ORDER **I & II**</u>
By **CA$H & Coffee**
<u>LOVE KNOWS NO BOUNDARIES **I II & III**</u>
By **Coffee**
<u>RAISED AS A GOON I, II, III & IV</u>
<u>BRED BY THE SLUMS I, II, III</u>
<u>BLAST FOR ME I & II</u>
<u>ROTTEN TO THE CORE I III</u>
<u>A BRONX TALE I, II, III</u>
<u>DUFFEL BAG CARTEL I II</u>
By **Ghost**
<u>LAY IT DOWN **I & II**</u>
<u>LAST OF A DYING BREED</u>
<u>BLOOD STAINS OF A SHOTTA I & II</u>

174

Lipstick Killah 3

By **Jamaica**
LOYAL TO THE GAME
LOYAL TO THE GAME II
LOYAL TO THE GAME III
LIFE OF SIN
By **TJ & Jelissa**
BLOODY COMMAS I & II
SKI MASK CARTEL I II & III
KING OF NEW YORK I II,III IV
RISE TO POWER I II
COKE KINGS
By **T.J. Edwards**
IF LOVING HIM IS WRONG...I & II
LOVE ME EVEN WHEN IT HURTS I II
By **Jelissa**
WHEN THE STREETS CLAP BACK I & II III
By **Jibril Williams**
A DISTINGUISHED THUG STOLE MY HEART I II & III
LOVE SHOULDN'T HURT I II III
RENEGADE BOYS I & II
By **Meesha**
A GANGSTER'S CODE I &, II III
By **J-Blunt**
PUSH IT TO THE LIMIT
By **Bre' Hayes**
BLOOD OF A BOSS **I, II, III, IV, V**
By **Askari**

THE STREETS BLEED MURDER **I, II & III**

THE HEART OF A GANGSTA I II& III

By **Jerry Jackson**

CUM FOR ME

CUM FOR ME 2

CUM FOR ME 3

CUM FOR ME 4

An **LDP Erotica Collaboration**

BRIDE OF A HUSTLA **I II & II**

THE FETTI GIRLS **I, II& III**

CORRUPTED BY A GANGSTA I, II & III

By **Destiny Skai**

WHEN A GOOD GIRL GOES BAD

By **Adrienne**

THE COST OF LOYALTY

By Kweli

A GANGSTER'S REVENGE **I II III & IV**

THE BOSS MAN'S DAUGHTERS

THE BOSS MAN'S DAUGHTERS II

THE BOSSMAN'S DAUGHTERS III

THE BOSSMAN'S DAUGHTERS IV

THE BOSS MAN'S DAUGHTERS **V**

A SAVAGE LOVE **I & II**

BAE BELONGS TO ME I II

A HUSTLER'S DECEIT I, II, III

WHAT BAD BITCHES DO I, II, III

By **Aryanna**

A KINGPIN'S AMBITON

A KINGPIN'S AMBITION **II**

I MURDER FOR THE DOUGH

By **Ambitious**

TRUE SAVAGE

TRUE SAVAGE II

TRUE SAVAGE **III**

TRUE SAVAGE **IV**

TRUE SAVAGE **V**

TRUE SAVAGE **VI**

By **Chris Green**

A DOPEBOY'S PRAYER

By **Eddie "Wolf" Lee**

THE KING CARTEL **I, II & III**

By **Frank Gresham**

THESE NIGGAS AIN'T LOYAL **I, II & III**

By **Nikki Tee**

GANGSTA SHYT **I II &III**

By **CATO**

THE ULTIMATE BETRAYAL

By **Phoenix**

BOSS'N UP **I , II & III**

By **Royal Nicole**

I LOVE YOU TO DEATH

By Destiny J

I RIDE FOR MY HITTA

I STILL RIDE FOR MY HITTA

Mimi

By **Misty Holt**

LOVE & CHASIN' PAPER

By **Qay Crockett**

TO DIE IN VAIN

SINS OF A HUSTLA

By **ASAD**

BROOKLYN HUSTLAZ

By **Boogsy Morina**

BROOKLYN ON LOCK I & II

By **Sonovia**

GANGSTA CITY

By **Teddy Duke**

A DRUG KING AND HIS DIAMOND I & II III

A DOPEMAN'S RICHES

HER MAN, MINE'S TOO I, II

CASH MONEY HO'S

By Nicole Goosby

TRAPHOUSE KING **I II & III**

KINGPIN KILLAZ I II III

STREET KINGS

PAID IN BLOOD

By **Hood Rich**

LIPSTICK KILLAH **I, II, III**

CRIME OF PASSION I & II

By **Mimi**

STEADY MOBBN' **I, II**

By **Marcellus Allen**

WHO SHOT YA **I, II**
Renta
GORILLAZ IN THE BAY **I II**
DE'KARI
TRIGGADALE
Elijah R. Freeman
GOD BLESS THE TRAPPERS I, II, III
THESE SCANDALOUS STREETS I, II, III
FEAR MY GANGSTA I, II, III
THESE STREETS DON'T LOVE NOBODY I, II
BURY ME A G I, II, III, IV, V
A GANGSTA'S EMPIRE I, II, III
Tranay Adams
THE STREETS ARE CALLING
Duquie Wilson
MARRIED TO A BOSS… I II
By Destiny Skai & Chris Green
KINGS OF THE GAME I II
Playa Ray

Mimi

BOOKS BY LDP'S CEO, CA$H

TRUST IN NO MAN

TRUST IN NO MAN 2

TRUST IN NO MAN 3

BONDED BY BLOOD

SHORTY GOT A THUG

THUGS CRY

THUGS CRY 2

THUGS CRY 3

TRUST NO BITCH

TRUST NO BITCH 2

TRUST NO BITCH 3

TIL MY CASKET DROPS

RESTRAINING ORDER

RESTRAINING ORDER 2

IN LOVE WITH A CONVICT

Coming Soon

BONDED BY BLOOD 2

BOW DOWN TO MY GANGSTA

Lipstick Killah 3